Carthage

By the same Author

Pasiphae

First published in the UK in 2003 by
Dewi Lewis Publishing
8 Broomfield Road
Heaton Moor
Stockport SK4 4ND
+44 (0)161 442 9450

www.dewilewispublishing.com

ISBN: 1-899235-29-9

Design & artwork production: Dewi Lewis Publishing
Printed and bound in Great Britain by
Biddles Ltd, Guildford and King's Lynn

9   8   7   6   5   4   3   2   1

Carthage
Peter Huby

DEWI LEWIS
PUBLISHING

Rome

1

They are crushed together in the tunnel. The playwright cannot see. What he can hear is muffled by the helmet strapped to his head. The helmet has no visor through which he might see. The grotesque metal mask has no eyeholes. A clown's face is painted on the blind visor. He sobs in his private darkness, his lungs dilating in little jerky spasms. He has wet himself. The warm smell of shit comes to him and for a moment he thinks it is his own smell. One of the other wretches in the stifling tunnel has fouled himself. Thoughts crowd in, running like fugitives among the terrors of the moment. He grips the heavy sword in his left hand and the round shield in his right. He has never held a sword before. The playwright knows in his bowels that he is going to die in the next few minutes but it means nothing. It is only a fragment in the cauldron of the instant.

He is borne suddenly forward by the weight of bodies, skidding and stumbling on the wet stones. He is jabbed viciously in the back. There is hot sand beneath his bare feet. Spots of light dance below his nose. The heat of the sun is on his back and the noise of the crowd fills his darkness like the roaring of surf.

Scipio Aemilianus is bored. Behind him in the box his sister Clodia is playing draughts with one of the slaves. She sits with her back to the arena and will not be persuaded to watch. He stretches in his seat and takes a sliver of ice from the gilt wine bucket by his feet. He crunches the ice. The debris in the arena is being cleared away, sand scattered over the blood. Buffoons belabour a donkey and girls with baskets are throwing lottery tickets into the crowd. He stretches and turns to his companion.

'Terentius Afer, why is it always so boring? It's not the blood that bothers me, it's the boredom.'

'Don't ask me. I'm just an Aventine pansy. I watch my feet most of the time. It's all too gross. I watch the crowd and that's pretty awful.'

Aemilianus guffaws.

'Look at this. I ask you?'

The gates have opened and the *andabatae* stumble into the arena, largely unnoticed by the crowd. In this interval between the main events the slopes of the stands seethe like termite hills. Dense files of bodies move in and out of the latrine exits. Vendors edge along the rows with programmes, wine, water, paper parasols, sherbet, rattles, chicken legs, whistles, badges. Bookies stand on the seats wearing large hats and holding their sticks of betting slips above their heads, shouting the odds, inaudible above the roar.

In the arena below, the blind warriors, locked into their eyeless helmets, flail and spin and run about. The playwright runs and runs until he crashes head first into the heavy posts of the barrier at the far side of the arena. He is dimly aware of the laughter of the crowd above him as he crouches foetus-like, stunned. Slaves with long spiked poles goad the sightless wretches toward one another. The blind men whirl and slash and dodge. A lucky blow takes off an arm below the elbow and the mutilated man grovels about on his knees searching for his severed limb. A thin fellow falls over him and they roll about in a frenzy of slashing and tearing. The one armed man staggers to his feet clutching his amputated arm, away from his butchered foe, and is instantly knocked over again. The slaves herd the wandering figures together, pushing them at one another. The ensuing conflicts are sudden panic stricken affairs. The blindly flailing blades produce weird slashed wounds. A diagonal sweep has emptied the entrails of a thick set man and the blue looped coils of his insides smoke on the sand at his feet while he stands clutching the place where his belly was. The metal mask of his helmet grins toothily. It really is very funny and the crowd are beginning to take an interest. Behind you! they shout, drolly.

A slave runs over to where the playwright lies and jabs him to his feet with the spike of his pole. He is herded back across the sand like a cow and comes up against the back of the stocky fellow with the spilled entrails. Their helmets clang against one another like buckets. The playwright hugs the broad back. He has lost his weapons. Spilled entrails does not react and they stand together swaying. Around them the numbers are dwindling. The blind men lie hacked and groaning, dying in the stifling privacy of their locked helmets while the crowd consult their programmes.

A last fight catches the attention of the front rows. The

combatants are holding each other with a free hand while they chop at one another with their swords. The damage they have inflicted is extensive. Both figures are scarlet from head to foot and the blood sprays into the air with each blow. The blows come more slowly. Dying is making them drowsy.

'Look. Look at those two.'

Aemilianus tugs at Terentius' sleeve. He winces as his glance takes in the scattered carnage and the two crimson men taking weary turns at hacking one another's flesh.

'Which one is Rome and which is Carthage, would you say?'

Terentius must watch, he cannot help himself. The blows come slower and slower, action draining toward inaction, exhaustion. The two sword arms waver uselessly. The sand is stained red in a great circle around them. A leg begins to shake violently and they both go down together, dying very quickly in each other's arms. A few yards away in another private darkness the playwright feels the broad back of spilled entrails begin to sink down. He releases his grip and the dead man falls. The playwright is still standing. He has no weapons. He has not struck a blow. He is unharmed, while the rest are dead or dying. Those in the crowd who have been following the detail, are tickled pink. There is a nudging and a pointing and word begins to spread. The little bloke in the grinning helmet in the middle has not struck a blow and he is the last man standing. There are ripples of laughter along the terraces. The joke takes a hundred paths and in a matter of moments there is laughter on the upper tiers.

At the very lip of the cauldron, on the uppermost tier of benches sits a sailor, the skipper of the *Osiris* out of Carthage. It is his first time at the games and he is overwhelmed. He cannot speak. His friend the furrier, who has a business in Rome, is eating dates and spitting out the stones absently as he marks his bets in the programme. A small child sitting under the bench below is watching the arrival of the date stones and is picking them up and arranging them in rows.

Chanting begins here and there, whistling and catcalls. Release him. Release him. The voice of the crowd grows huge, becomes the voice of the ocean. The sound surges in great dark waves, the voice of the people. Among the senators of Rome there is a saying: in the arena the mob has the Consulate. Out along the Via Flaminia, ten miles from the city, Cato cranes out of the curtains of his litter and listens to the distant roar.

The playwright feels the roaring in his chest. He is a blank, a zero, an absence. He is the sound of roaring surf. Suddenly hard hands are holding him and he feels the scrape of the key in the lock at the back of his helmet. The metal casque comes away and he cannot see anything in the brilliant light.

'Look!'

'What?' Terentius is reluctant to look again.

'The little man. Him. It's him.'

'Who?'

'The playwright. I could swear it's the playwright.'

Aemilianus is aware of his little sister standing at his shoulder. Clodia is watching the small blood-soaked man blinking in the sunshine, standing like a clown in his crimson motley. She can make nothing in thought of what she sees or how she feels.

'What? What is it?'

'You remember. When we went to the theatre. The play was called *The General*. It made us all laugh and your uncle said there'll be trouble, and the man who wrote the play came out on to the stage at the end and the crowd clapped. We think this is him.'

'But it was funny. It made us all laugh. Why is he here?'

2

'The war with Hannibal? I was a little girl when he first came over the mountains from the North. The city was empty in those days. The men had gone, all of them. They had gone to fight Hannibal. There were piles of rubbish on the streets. There was no one to do the work. The public gardens were overgrown. You could look down the Argiletum and not see a man, just women and children. There were old men. Your great-grandfather came to stay. He came from his estate in the country. I remember the smell of him. It was the smell of camphor, mothballs. He looked like an actor in his old-fashioned army uniform. He went to the Forum in the mornings, him and the other old men. They burned a lot of shops, businesses belonging to Carthaginians. I liked the Carthaginians when I was a little girl. I liked their earrings and their long tunics. Yids. Gugga bastards. That's what your grandfather called them. When Hannibal came out of the mountains they closed up their shops and left. Some stayed. I remember the names above the shops changing. They changed them so that people wouldn't know that they were Carthaginians. There was a fabric shop just off the Via Tusculana with great big flags of floaty gauze outside in all the colours you could think of. I remember. On the little square with the old temple.'

The old woman falls silent and Clodia pauses a moment, the hairbrush resting in her grandmother's hair. The fine white hair clicks and sparks, flies out away from the old woman's head. The girl loves to take out the big gold pins and let the ghostly halo fall loose and wild, loves to watch it fly out in points that flicker bluely in the lamplight as she brushes and brushes, forgetting to count the strokes, growing dreamy and absent. Often, when she has been brushing for a while, her grandmother begins to speak, taking up some part of her long and private story. It can begin anywhere; the old woman's nightly reordering of her past. Memory breaks the surface into speech unexpectedly. Sometimes the old woman returns to the same memories for nights together, turning the recollection this way and that until, as if satisfied, she passes on. Tonight the ground is familiar.

'The temple, what was its name?'

The girl pulls the brush down through the white gossamer.

'The Venus Victrix.'

'That's it. The Venus Victrix.'

Clodia begins to brush again, waiting for her grandmother to find the thread of her memory. The silence extends, measured by the faint sound of the brush strokes and the clicking sparks. Sometimes the old woman slips into sleep, the straight patrician shoulders ebbing little by little toward a crone's bent profile, but tonight she is alert. The story starts again, from a different place.

'The wounded came in on carts. We used to watch from the walls. I would go down with Statia, one of the Spanish slaves, when we were supposed to be shopping in the market. The line of carts seemed to go on forever. When the city hospitals were full, they put up tents outside the walls. It looked like a fair, all those pavilions and marquees. Well-off families gave them up for the war effort. Your great grandfather gave away the striped one that we used to take to Baie for the summer. I flew to my mother in tears when they took it away. You could see it from the walls, even among all the others. It was pink and white, with a valance and when it was on the beach at Baie there were little pennants on the tops of the poles. They seemed to have forgotten to put the pennants up. She took me down to the tents one day, my mother. It was muddy among the tents and there were men everywhere. It was frightening to see so many men when they had all been gone for so long. They seemed strange, like dark animals, wolves.'

The old woman falls silent, leaving the slight, regular sound of the brush in the room, and the girl wonders if she has lost her way again in the labyrinth.

'It had a boot on. I thought it *was* a boot at first, standing at the door of the tent for the slaves to clean, but it was a leg, a man's leg. You could see the white bone at the top and the veins. The skin was blue and dirty. Just inside the tent flap there were piles of arms and legs. I had a basket of fruit for the wounded and I dropped it and the oranges rolled out into the red mud. My mother wouldn't let me pick them up. I cried and cried because our stripy tent was full of arms and legs.'

Clodia can feel her grandmother's shoulders begin to tremble.

'Tell me about the shop, the fabric shop. Tell me about the floaty gauze.'

The next night as Clodia brushes the old woman's hair; Cornelia takes up her thread as if there had been no pause, as if no time at all had passed since she spoke last.

'He came, you know. Later, years later. He came and sat on his horse outside the Colline gate. I was a grown girl then, full grown, and he came, riding out of my dreams.'

Her grandmother's hands stray uncertainly to her throat, to her empty dugs, a young girl mysteriously betrayed by the years.

'Who came?'

'Hannibal. It was the summer. I had on my summer dress. We were standing with the crowds on the city wall. Everyone knew that the Carthaginian army was only a few miles away. The ramparts were crowded with people, thousands and thousands of them, women, slaves, foreigners, old people, cripples, lining the city wall where the road comes in from Latium, all waiting. I was afraid. I could feel the fear, running like threads of flame in my bowels. They were so quiet, those thousands of people, just waiting. I had Lucius your great uncle with me. He was just a tiny boy then. He's dead now. He died of a fever in Spain when he was a tribune with the army.

And then you could see the dust, a line on the horizon. Hannibal came out of the dust on his horse. He rode up to the city through the dry fields in that hot afternoon and sat there on his horse below the walls, a dusty man with an eye patch. He sat quite still in the hot afternoon sun without even a hat, while behind him his cavalry drew up in lines, dusty, tired men on thin horses. There were no elephants, no shining armour, no splendour, just long lines of dusty, dark eyed men on matted horses. I held up your uncle in my arms and I whispered in his ear, 'Look, look, there is Hannibal,' and I pointed with my outstretched arm. Little Lucius whimpered and wet himself. I felt the hot piss through my dress. Hannibal looked up. It must have been the movement of my arm. He looked up at the crowded battlements and I can remember it now. He looked up toward me, this one eyed man who had killed my father, who had slaughtered so many sons and husbands, who had cut off all those arms and legs, this ogre, this monster from my weeping childish dreams. He looked into my face. He saw me and my loins grew liquid. I was wet and it ran down between my thighs. I thought for a minute that I'd wet myself like little Lucius.

Clodia's brush stops in mid sweep, her hand trembling. The old woman's stare is unfocussed. She is reaching, aching toward some resolution, some perfection. At last she sighs, gives over, relinquishes the moment. Clodia begins to brush again, hesitant and agitated. The old woman speaks once more.

'I was a virgin. I did not know what it meant. I never knew. Not ever.'

Clodia has an aunt, a widow, an unbending matron of the old school. Her aunt has a summer residence near Tivoli, a day's journey from Rome. The house stands among olive groves on the slopes of the Tiburtine hills above the town. Her aunt visits the house from time to time to take the waters in the town spa. The rank sulphurous water is good for her women's complaint. It is understood that her niece is her companion on these visits.

The house looks over the plain towards Rome and Clodia idles through long afternoons among the stepped and terraced lawns gazing out over the heat shimmer, trying without success to read Xenophon's *Cyropaedeia*, a gift from her brother, her adopted brother, while her aunt patrols the house and the kitchen garden. The house slaves dread these visits.

In the silence of the night Clodia leaves her stifling room and descends to the garden again. The cypresses stand tall in the blue grey mist and the moon is white and round, waxing toward the full out over the vague vistas of the plain. The air is still and hot. Somewhere on a distant farm a dog barks. The girl moves among the olive trees, her toes treading last year's unpicked olives. Moonlight passes in white bars across her flesh as she moves naked among the shadows of the trees in the dark sea swell of the loss that is desire. She moves among crimson visions of Hannibal the butcher. She cannot distinguish in these voluptuous waking dreams the butcher of Carthage from her memories of the arena, of the last man standing, bloodied and blinded and helpless.

Clodia gets down from her aunt's carriage where the Vicus Iugarius passes the end of the Forum and walks with her slave from there to her home on the Palatine. It is late in the day and sparrows drive like noisy leaves across the empty Forum. A gang of road layers is working late resetting an expanse of cobbles. They kneel, raking up the sand with the picks of their hammers and tapping the stones home and level with practised panache. They sing and shout to one another or curse their labourers cheerfully.

In the city of Rome there is building work going on everywhere. Bricks and crates of sawn stone are stacked on every street corner it seems, and the skyline is a forest of scaffolding. The streets are dusty and littered with builders' debris. The Forum itself has been a building site for as long as Clodia can remember. There are new temples in the city, market halls, fountains, a new hospital on the island, new houses for the rich among the pines of the Palatine. She hardly thinks about these things, is unaware of the revenues of conquest flowing unseen into the city, which are making this transformation of the city possible.

The city is full of Greeks and that too is all she has known in her fifteen years, Greek architects, sculptors, stonemasons, slaves. Everyone who is anyone has a Greek slave or a Greek tutor. Men shave their faces in the Greek manner and Athenian couture is all the rage. Among the plebs of the Suburra has grown a half-formed resentment of all things Greek. Too many Greeks in the city, taking our jobs, too many dirty foreigners. They should go back where they came from. There are stock jokes about Greeks usually involving sodomy and sex with animals. There are beatings and riots on hot summer nights. These popular resentments are exploited by politicians of the right wing, by old style republicans and new men.

The white disc of the full moon is already rising between the tall trunks of the umbrella pines and there is a sound of roosting starlings as the two women make their way up the stepped streets of the Palatine. The torches are lit along the steep secluded thoroughfares. Outside the gates of an exclusive residence a night watchman is raking cold embers from his brazier.

It is quite dark when she enters her grandmother's room. Cornelia has waved away the slave who came with a taper to light the lamps. In the darkness Clodia takes up the ivory backed hairbrush. She works with only the flicker of faint blue light in the halo of the old woman's hair to see by. Cornelia's voice sounds younger in the darkness, young and firm.

'It was a strange day. Such a hot strange day.'

A breathless avidity catches in the girl's throat. She brushes for a moment, waiting, before she must ask.

'What day, grandmother?'

The old woman's eyes flick up, knowing and amused.

'Which day do you think? The day Hannibal came with his one

eye and sat on his horse below me, while my summer dress billowed out in the hot wind.'

The vision fills the darkness in the room. The girl is high up and the flimsy dress loops away from her naked limbs while the one eyed butcher sits below on his sweating horse and watches her.

'Of course, it didn't billow in the wind at all. I was hemmed in by the crowds. My dress had no room to blow about and besides, the day was hot and windless, but that's the story I told myself, that my summer dress blew away from my body as I stood above the one eyed man. It became a sort of dream, not a memory at all.

He seemed to sit there for a great while. It was as if he had fallen into a reverie, there in the baking sun, with all those thousands of pairs of eyes watching him. And it was so quiet. No one spoke. At last he looked up like someone waking from sleep, turned his horse and walked it back through the lines of his cavalry and as he passed through their ranks the horsemen turned to follow. It was a lovely thing to see. By four and four they turned to follow him, like so many shadows, orderly and silent, moving off in a great column. The dust rose up from the dry earth and they moved away like riders in a dream, until all you could see was a distant cloud moving toward the horizon, and we knew that we were delivered.

That night my mother went out to the temple. We all went, my mother, my aunt, me, and even some of the slave women. In those days of the war, with the city empty of men, the women did as they pleased, went out when they pleased. My grandfather fumed and shouted but my mother just smiled and took a torch down from the bracket on the wall. On the streets there were women everywhere, making their way to the temples, carrying their own torches. We went to the temple of Cybele, the Mother. I remember standing in the darkness with the smell of incense and the torchlight glinting in the polished stone and the feeling of dark space above. My mother pushed back the hood of her cloak and took out the pins from her hair and unbraided it, so that it fell in a great mane about her shoulders and down her back. She put her two hands to the back of her neck and threw her hair forward over her face. I felt strange and frightened, seeing her like that. She knelt down on the stones of the temple and she began to sweep the floor with her hair. All around

15

me, women began letting their hair fall loose. They were kneeling forward as if they might be weeping, brushing the stones of the floor with their hair. And it was the same all over the city, in all of the temples. Women were sweeping the floors of the temples with their hair.'

3

Cato is opening his mail in the atrium of his villa, his feet on Aphrodite's tessellated bosom. He tears open the wax seals irritably and drops the letters to the mosaic floor after a cursory glance at their contents. He stumps through into the wide, sparsely furnished living room, still clutching the last of the letters. He has not eaten and his temper is short. His temper is always short when he is hungry. The house slaves are wary. He sits and they come forward with a table and his meal, struggling for invisibility.

'Do you know what this is?'

He catches a flinching houseboy by the ear and waves the letter beneath his nose.

'Of course you don't. It's an invitation. It's an invitation to an evening of philosophical discussion! Pah! Philosophical discussion, my arse. It'll be full of Greeks, subversives, revolutionaries. They're all the same. What do Romans want with philosophy? In Rome we have the rules, tradition, respect. Send 'em back where they came from, damned shirt-lifters. It's the same here. It's the same in Rome. It's an infection, a canker. You know, there are rich young faggots in the city who'll pay the price of a farm for a good-looking slave to bugger. In the Forum too, in my basilica, with their painted faces and their shaved legs. I tell them. I make no bones about it. Buggers, sodomites, the lot of you.'

The old man pushes the youth away and begins to eat. Fragments of food spray across the table as he fulminates grumpily to himself. In the shadows slaves roll their eyes as he mumbles and curses his way through his meal.

Against the marble door post, just out of Cato's line of sight,

16

stands the Armenian, heron-still, his shaved head aglint in the shadows. Harpax has been Cato's secretary for half a lifetime. He organises the old man's public life, writes his letters, composes his speeches, corrects the spelling in the spidery drafts of his books, measures his moods. He even shares the old man's passion for gardening. He began years ago by affecting to share his master's enthusiasm for horticulture out of an instinct for his own advancement, but over the seasons appearance has grown into reality. These days, time not spent in the flower gardens or the nurseries has become mere irritation. Their abiding enthusiasm is for the cultivation of figs.

Harpax is a slave, though his servile status in the household has grown transparent. The younger slaves don't believe it, scorning the idea that this aloof personage, about whom clings no hint of servile deference, is just another of the old bully's chattels.

He was sold to Cato by Carthaginian slave traders on the harbour side at Ostia, on his seventeenth birthday. The voyage had been bad. The cargo was largely dead on arrival. The slave galley scraped at its moorings and its foetor lifted the gut. The slaves that had survived were going cheap, and Cato was never able to pass up a bargain.

The skinny youth was put to work in the kitchens, but his quickness, his memory for figures, his silent compliance, marked him out, and he was moved in with the scribes and secretaries. His rise to indispensability had been invisible and inexorable. After ten years, on their return from the Spanish campaign, in the grandiloquent days after his triumph, Cato had offered the Armenian *manumission*, freedom. He had waved the folded bronze wafer, the *manumission* seal, in his face. 'Take it. Be a free man.' Harpax bowed, asked for time to think. He lay in his narrow cot that night, his eyes open in the darkness, knowing that the only freedom he craved was the freedom to be another's dog. To be the servant is to be the master. Cato never raised the matter again. That was thirty years ago.

Harpax watches the old man eat, waiting for his moment, watching for the sullen brow to lift, waiting for the belch or the fart of repletion. In his days as magistrate wretches were condemned in haste so that Cato could dine the sooner. Pardons were commoner in

the early afternoons. Defence lawyers paid heavy bribes to the court
ushers for a slot after lunch when red faced, ranting Cato was on the
bench.

The old man farts loudly, and sighs. Harpax moves into the room.
He stands before the old man watching him pour water into the
vinegary wine he still insists on drinking, out of some regard for his
forgotten reputation as an old soldier of Spartan habits. Cato looks up.

'Wine?'

Harpax demurs and takes a seat across from his master. He
unpacks the contents of his folder. Cato sits picking his teeth. He
farts again with a perceptible raising of a buttock and a slight wince.
Harpax passes over a document.

'This is a list of your fellow senators who will be travelling with
you on the embassy to Carthage.'

Cato continues to pick his teeth thoughtfully.

'Did you fix the bastard who wrote the play?'

'Yes. It's all taken care of.'

Cato adjusts the distance so that he can read the names, holding
the parchment almost at arm's length. After a moment he stabs his
forefinger at a name.

'Scipio Nasica! A damned pacifist, that one. Can't be trusted to
take a firm line with the Yids. You should have heard him in the
Senate. Some Greek philosophical nonsense. What was he saying
now? Ah yes, ...the state needs an external adversary in order to
maintain its own stability. Something like that. Did you ever hear
such ballocks?'

He tosses the parchment down.

'The others are sound enough.'

Harpax passes him another sheet.

'This is the schedule. You travel in your personal litter to Rome
tomorrow. The official barge leaves for Ostia on Wednesday and the
squadron makes the crossing to Africa the day after. Once there, the
delegation will be housed in a suite adjoining the Carthaginian
Senate House.'

'What's on the agenda this time?'

'On the Carthaginian agenda... the usual things. The grain
arrangements for the legions serving in Greece. The usual request for
permission to rearm, to re-establish an army. It seems that the

18

Numidians are causing them trouble again. This year they make the last of the reparations payments the Senate imposed after the war with Hannibal. It's fifty years since the war ended. They'll be expecting some kind of official response to that. Something conciliatory.'

'Conciliatory, my arse. What else? What have we got?'

'There is still pressure from the trade guilds. The merchants' delegations to the people's tribune are insisting they need tariffs to protect them from Carthaginian imports. It's the standard Roman merchants' lament about Carthage. Sharp practice, substandard goods, secret cartels, and so on.'

'So, what's the line? What's the word from the civil service?'

'The war ended fifty years ago. The Carthaginians have kept to their side of the peace treaty, more or less. Rome has to decide if Carthage is still the enemy.'

'I don't trust the buggers, personally, and the merchants in Rome are right, they are wily devils, but I prefer them to the Greeks, and we've spared the Greeks their cities, mostly. You know, when I was serving as Consul to the army in Spain I sacked a city for every week I was there.'

Harpax has heard that line, that lie, a hundred times. Latterly the old man seems to have forgotten that he was there too, seems not to remember that Harpax was his orderly throughout. The Armenian remembers the burning villages, the mass crucifixions, the deportations of whole districts. He does not remember any Homeric sacking of cities. He remembers lines of starving peasants being led into slavery. He remembers the smell. He also remembers how that smell made him weep, for it was the smell of the people of his own village, so long ago, when the Carthaginian slavers came for them with their chains and their branding irons, when he was sixteen. Smells, Harpax thinks, summon up the past too strongly. They conjure grief, darkness.

'So what do you think...?'

The old man puts a hand on each knee and looks at his Armenian squarely.

'You know a thing or two about foreign policy. This Carthage question needs an agreed line, a definite strategy. What do you think? What's your opinion?'

19

The Armenian looks for a moment into some middle distance.

'About Carthage? I am of the opinion that Carthage should be destroyed.'

Cato picks his teeth in silence until he disinters the offending fragment. He tries to focus on the particle that clings to the toothpick, then says,

'I heard it said that a million people live in Greater Carthage.'

4

The Rome riverfront is an unkempt sweep of wharves and warehouses on the bend of the Tiber. In the moonlight it is deserted. Hanno the Carthaginian is drunk, but he tells himself it's just that his land legs haven't returned to him yet after the long months at sea. Is that what I am telling myself, he asks himself. Am I lying? Am I just drunk? Behind him the noisy, yellow tavern glare recedes and he finds himself walking on echoing cobbles in the deserted darkness. Never was much of a tavern, in Hanno's opinion, the *Poseidon*, full of scowling Roman lightermen making the sign of the eye. In fact he doesn't altogether care for the port of Rome. Not a place for ear-ringed Carthaginians.

It occurs to him that he is not quite sure where his ship is. He is not sure of very much. Yesterday he went to the games, his first time. The memory rises up within him like shame. He shakes his head to be rid of the recollection. Despite himself, he sees the tiny puppets hacking and slashing on the white medallion of sand. A small man in an iron mask standing foolishly and blind in a bright butcher's yard, a sole survivor. The chanting surges like surf across the packed terraces. He sees the small man standing like a helpless angel among the quartered carcasses. It had never occurred to Hanno to be frightened of the Romans until yesterday. He is frightened of them now.

He cannot think where his ship is berthed and it makes him laugh out loud. Gugga skipper loses ship (in port). He can see it now, daubed on some brothel wall. He comes to a halt, trying to gather his wits, get his bearings, laughing foolishly to himself. He scans the impenetrable forest of masts that stretches away along the creaking nightblack wharf. This is Rome. Should be better organised, better lit, he thinks. Piss poor arrangement, he thinks. In Carthage the harbours are lit every night at the public expense, end to end. Watchmen sit before their braziers every few hundred yards. Beacons burn at the harbour mouth as a guide for incoming ships. He has seen them a score of times, those twin points of light appearing on the night black horizon. The port of Rome, on the other hand, he thinks, is a wasteland where a law abiding Punic skipper might well get his throat cut, particularly after winning money dicing with thuggish lightermen. He glances back toward the fogged glimmer of the tavern.

He wanders out unsteadily from beneath the shadows of the warehouses across the moonlit cobbles toward the dark ranks of ships. He steps over jumbled hawsers as he finds his way along the wharf beneath each high prow. *Bireme* out of Dalmatia. Egyptian oiler. Tyrian galley, ready for the breaker's yard by the look of it. Even in the darkness Hanno's knowledge of these things is absolute, though he cannot find his own ship. He cannot find the *Osiris*, cannot quite remember where on this endless river front his ship is berthed, and it makes him giggle. Above him a swarthy face curses and spits. 'I cannot think straight, you dago bastard, because I am drunk, and because I need a piss.' Hanno will not do it there, in the open, even in the darkness. He stumbles back toward the black wall of warehouses and finds a stygian alley. Piss splatters noisily against the invisible wall and he leans his forehead against the cool stone and sighs. He closes his eyes... and blinks them open again to stop the world turning.

Something clammy enters his consciousness. His dilated brain spins down to a black iris. Sobriety is instant. He is not alone in the alley. To his right another entity breathes. He wonders if all final moments are this simple. He can picture his knife on the shelf of the cabin in the stern of his ship that he may never see again.

He slows his movements, adjusting his breech clout with a mundane, strange deliberation, bending his knees all the while until his head is at waist height, and then goes, as hard and fast as he can, to the right.

His feet skid on greasy refuse and his head crashes into the unseen body, driving it along the wall and down among the piled rubbish. He is on top of his assailant, flailing for fists and knives. He finds the throat. There is a bloom of perfume, tremors in the flesh. His calloused fingers inch up the strangely fragile neck and into the hair. The scented darkness blooms afresh, heavy and troubling: no stale whorehouse odour, this. He is aware of the slightness of the body crushed beneath his weight. His hand finds the flimsy hem and his fingers push upward along the slender naked thigh, finds the wet furrow. The trembling body convulses. Confusion rises in the sailor like fear and he moves suddenly as if he would get to his feet. Girlish fingers grip his arms. 'Do it! Do it!' The Latin is pure, aristocratic. Hanno has a Carthaginian's ear for these things. She cries out like a falcon as he enters her.

5

The last man standing is smiling in the sun. He is blinking in the dazzle as his head turns. Clodia is standing by Aemilianus in the box watching him as he searches the crowd with his eyes. She is standing by her adopted brother with a piece from the game of draughts in her hand, waiting for the last man, waiting for the travel of his gaze to pass across her. She aches for the travelling gaze, for the passing of the cloud shadow and the sunlight of his blinking stare, tense with expectancy. The beacon intensity of his gaze finds her at last and refulgent warmth wells up inside her. Engulfing white light petals in her loins.

She wakes in the passing of the spasm, lies quietly in its aftermath. She comes to herself little by little as she lies unmoving, her face against the pillow. Flowers are scattered across the marble floor and last night's dress is in a heap. The drift of faded flowers, roses, violets, white lilies, is what is left of the bouquets that came with the carrier from Tusculum yesterday for the Kalends. Yesterday? How placid she was, how uncomplicated, in that simple faraway time, dressing the little shrine in the atrium for the Kalends of May. She sees herself as in a little mirror, reflected out of some distant past, arranging the white lilies.

She hears a light cart entering the courtyard below, the sound of grit crushed beneath the wheel's rim, the confusion of hooves. She turns onto her back in the bed and winces. The flesh of her hip and shoulder is grazed and bruised. The memory of the dark alleyway comes and goes like the recollection of a shopping list. The mad heat of the flesh has cooled to forgetfulness, ebbed, banished itself to the waiting deep. She has woken to her daylight self, taken up her girlish disguise like a garment.

She stands before the mirror and the grazed flesh shows surprisingly against the whiteness of her skin. The bruises have a greenish cast. Her hands are still dirty and there is dirt beneath her fingernails. She brushes the faint whitish flakes of memory from her inner thigh as she turns in the mirror's critical gaze. Outside in the sunlit courtyard, voices, and she catches the sound of Aemilianus' laughter.

He is standing by the fountain in a new uniform, turning slowly while his tailor kneels like a suppliant, his mouth full of pins, adjusting the hem.

'What do you think, little sister?'

He poses for her with a mock-heroic flourish. She is standing in the shadow of the colonnade clutching her robe to her throat. She is not his little sister and his familiarity touches some unnameable disdain in her. I am not your sister, she wants to shout, I am your cousin, your distant relation. He has been adopted into the family. It is what happens between rich families. When there is no male heir in a family then someone suitable is adopted. He is the new heir, will be the head of the family one day, another Scipio, another legend. He is already a legend in his own eyes, this arrogant person, this glib, over-familiar person, this man.

'What do you think?'

He sweeps the heavy military cloak dramatically around his body, burying the expostulating tailor in its folds.

'Are you going back to the army, back to Spain?'

She does not move from her place in the shadow.

'Spain? No, dear sister. If all of the rumours are true I shall be going to Carthage. I am to be military tribune to the Fourth Legion, the youngest in its history.'

'What will happen to him?'

'Happen to whom?'

'To the last man standing.'

'The last man standing?'

'At the games. The playwright. The play, *The General*. You remember.'

'I expect they'll put him back in the next time.'

'Back in?'

'Back into the arena.'

'But the crowd voted to spare him.'

'That was yesterday. Today, who remembers?'

She is appalled, speechless at this sudden overwhelming perfidy. It is too huge for speech. Her stomach cramps in the extremity of it. Her voice, finally, is a whisper.

'Put him back in?'

'Until somebody swipes his leg off, or his head.'

Her breath passes shallowly, in and out. The tailor has finished pinning up the tunic and he holds a mirror so that Aemilianus can inspect the results. The young man turns slowly, looking over his shoulder at the reflection of his hemline.

'Actually, that's not true. The new fleet is being fitted out. They'll be emptying the jails for the galleys. Your playwright will be going to Carthage I expect, like me.'

Carthage

6

Pigeons fly around inside the echoing dome of the library of Carthage. They coo and rotate on the tops of pilasters. An echoing susurration of whispering voices and scraping parchment rises into the void. It is the universal sound of all libraries. Below, the ranks of translators, scribes, copyists, editors, compilers, bend to their work. The rows of desks stretch in an uncountable multitude across the vast floor and figures move silently along the aisles with stacked trolleys of manuscripts.

It seems to Cato, as he stands among his delegation, white togas dwarfed against the tall bronze doors, that this sea of scribblers is far too wide. Such an overstated apparatus bespeaks a suspicious obsession with writing, he thinks, with the persuasive, the devious and corrupt, the altogether too subtle and sophisticated. He moves out irritably among the desks trailing an anxious gaggle of diplomats and library officials.

'What's going on? What are all these people actually doing?'

The chief librarian is in an ecstasy of anxiety.

'To your left is translation. We translate into and out of twenty three languages.'

'Translate what, exactly?'

The old man wanders along between the rows of desks, craning over the shoulders of apparently oblivious scribes. He stops to watch a pen flying over the parchment, the unfolding of a fluent trail of opaque symbols. The source document lies open, battered and mildewed, unintelligible. The chief librarian is at Cato's elbow. He clears his throat nervously. He is an administrator, bookish, reclusive, unused to managing irascible Roman dignitaries. He should have been told.

'This document is part of a series, documents relating to the upper Nile region. It is being translated into Punic. The source language is no longer written or spoken widely. The language was suppressed some hundreds of years ago by the Hyksos kings as part of their pacification programme'.

Cato's eyebrows migrate slowly up and down but his expression remains blank. He is out of his depth. He is troubled, oppressed by the mysteries of this arcane institution. Inwardly, unconsciously, he is awaiting a chance to fulminate. It is what he does well. His years at the bar have taught him that righteous indignation is a useful tool, a reliable podium from which to speak, especially when on unfamiliar ground. He moves on down the aisle as if he were inspecting troops, aware, in a satisfied sort of way, of the nervous train of officials behind him. The collective scratching of quill pens is loud. His eye catches the familiar square cut shapes of a Latin text.

'And this?'

Cato reaches in over the shoulder of the startled scribe and picks up the Latin document. The chief librarian's stomach lurches. The old man adjusts the distance of the parchment so that he can read the heading. 'The proceedings of the Campanian vintners guild.... ?' Cato looks up at the librarian, his eyebrows raised like the jaws of a trap. The librarian, bereft of choices, speaks in what he hopes are candid tones.

'These documents are publicly available in Rome. Our own wine growers take an interest in the activities of other wine growing nations.'

'An interest!' Cato has found his theme. His tone is incredulous, outraged. 'An interest! This is spying, espionage!'

The librarian's head is down. He knows his career is in ruins.

'Your Honour, please. This is routine work, what any commercial library engages in. We have a duty to keep our merchants and manufacturers properly informed.'

'Properly informed!'

The note of righteous rage is gauged to a nicety.

'Do you mean to tell me that you spy on everyone?'

'Your Honour, I beg you. This is a small part of our work. Over here we have literature, plays, sacred writing, medicine, engineering, agriculture... horticulture...'

'Horticulture?'

The librarian senses a gleam of light.

'Indeed. Come, come. Please'.

He leads the way between the desks, treading the knife-edge of his professional future.

'Here, for example, we have Mago. Mago's *Compendium of Horticulture* used to be in demand all over the world. We have translated it into Syriac, Greek, Hurrian. Mago himself is now dead. His estates outside Carthage were a model of good practice. His figs were world famous.'

'Figs? Figs, you say?'

The librarian has stumbled upon salvation.

'Indeed. Mago devotes a whole chapter to the cultivation of figs.'

'Has this book been translated into Latin?'

'I believe not, your Honour. Your countrymen have no great interest in translated texts, except for Greek plays, and pornography.'

'Can you have this, this whatshisname, translated?'

' Indeed. An honour, your Honour. The name is Mago.'

'Yes, but what's his name?'

'Mago, your honour.'

'That's the fellow. When can you have it done?'

'Six weeks. With the compliments of the city library.'

'Six weeks?'

A note of irritation has crept back into Cato's voice.

'We will do our utmost, your Honour. There are twenty-eight volumes. Is there some rush?'

Cato has regained his gravitas, having been betrayed momentarily by his own enthusiasm. He sneers icily at the cringing functionary.

'Who knows? The world may end. The sky may fall in. Carthage may slide into the sea.'

He turns, deploying the whole rhetoric of his purple hemmed toga, and stumps out of the place, trailing hangers-on as he goes.

7

The steep streets below the Byrsa are crowded with evening shoppers. The sky above the tall tenements is still red gold, but down in the street, torches and lamps are flickering into life among the stalls and shops. The scribe stops off to buy eggs, bread, oil. He buys figs on impulse, and he smiles to himself. He never eats figs. As he stands waiting for his change, tall hats pass behind him, a file of orthodox worshippers, zealots, threading their way through the narrow crowded thoroughfare, men and boys, holding elaborate scrolls of sacred text before them, wearing the long ringlets of their caste. The scribe passes between two stalls and turns up into a stepped alleyway.

He smells cat piss in the stairwell of his tenement as he trudges up the worn stairs with his shopping and he frowns to himself. He knows the cat. It belongs to the widow on the second floor. The old woman has put a collar round its neck with a little bronze nametag. Hadad. Hadad the cat is a stringy, insistent, supercilious creature, with a long Egyptian nose. Spendios reaches the top and elbows down the wooden latch of his door. Inside, the last rays of the sun spill across the floor. The shutters are drawn back and his mother is sitting on the narrow balcony which overlooks the street, doing her lacework. She is a birdlike shadow against the light, her bony fingers flickering across the bobbins.

'You're late. Why did you come that way? I saw you. Why did you come up the alley by the bakers? You never come that way.'

Spendios stands behind her on the balcony in the orange light and he kisses the back of her head. She tuts. Below, it is already dark and streetlamps are burning. Beyond the end of the street, he can see the last sunlight dancing minutely on the water of the harbour.

'There was a procession, Baal-Hammonites.'

She tuts.

'Holy Joes. That's what your father called them.'

'We should move from here.'

'At my time of life? I'm too old to move.'

29

'You're too old to stay. I'm fifty next month, God help me. All those stairs.'

'Do like I do. Stop on every landing, talk to your neighbours, be sociable.'

'When you talk to Mrs Whatshername, tell her to keep her cat off the stairs. The stairwell stinks.'

'Poor old soul. She's not been herself since she fell in the street last month.'

'What do you mean, poor old soul? You're older than she is.'

The old woman affects not to hear. He moves back into the room and sits at his table below the big square of orange sunlight on the wall. He likes to work through this hour at this time of year, beneath the patch of sunlight that migrates slowly into the room and across the wall, while the evening light in the room ebbs slowly, growing soft, suffused. In the winter the sun does not enter the apartment at all.

As well as his work as an official scribe at the library, Spendios takes on private work. It is mostly routine stuff, contracts, letters, bills of lading. It pays for his visits to the theatre and the concert hall with his mother. They go together to recitals, plays, poetry. They sit together: she tiny, birdlike, he big and hunched: sharing a bag of pistachio nuts. Sometimes they buy sugared almonds which they suck, she because she must, having few teeth left in her mouth, he because he does not want to be heard crunching in the quieter moments. She does not really like sugared almonds but she humours him. She believes that he has always had a weakness for sugared almonds, since he was a little boy. Spendios never really cared for sugared almonds, except when he was little. It is a small ritual misunderstanding, honed over the years, which brings obscure comfort to them both.

They sit together with their hands in their laps listening to the singers in the circle of lamps. They are singing the story of Aqhat the hunter and Anat the goddess. The goddess is offering the hunter immortality in exchange for his bow. The hunter is rejecting her offer, his arms and hands making the traditional gestures as he sings. Aqhat will die for his foolishness.

Spendios takes the work out of its folder and sharpens a pen. It is a contract of sale, four copies, for a property in the suburbs, in

30

Megara. Property prices are falling in the city. Families are selling up and moving away. Businesses are relocating in Alexandria, Delos, Sidon. Slaves are cheaper too. He has heard of cases of emigrating families casting unsaleable slaves adrift. They beg in the Agora. The streets are not safe. He pushes the work to one side and pulls his journal across the table. He opens it by the ebony bookmark, a polished wafer of wood, the red lettering of the inscription worn almost to nothing. It is the fragile totem of his calling, a gift given to him in childhood, a nodal, determining thing. He dips the pen in the ink and draws it out with the quick turning motion of the professional scribe. He inserts the date and begins to write in his fluent hand. He finds comfort in writing, in the flicker of the unfolding text. Punic is an elegant script. It gives him pleasure to write in his own language. He has never quite learned to like the blockish Latin which is his stock-in-trade. Translating out of Latin into Punic is like trying to weave chiffon from ships' hawsers. Latin he finds numb, incapable of nuance, fatally ambiguous, lacking precision, a blunt, obvious cudgel of a language. He writes,

> *The ambassadors from Rome are back in the city, having returned from the disputed lands along the Numidian border. Nothing has been said, no proclamation has been made, though it is obvious that the Romans will find in favour of the Numidian bandits. It is not a question of truth or justice. Their foreign policy demands it. They will not protect us. They will not allow us to protect ourselves. I believe the shadow of Hannibal still falls across the Roman mind. They are like children frightened of the dark.*
>
> *Today, Marcus Porcius Cato toured the library with other members of the delegation. He has asked for a translation of Mago's Horticulture into Latin, though why he should choose such a windy and second-rate work is a mystery. They are a strange people, like hammers.*

On impulse, he begins to write in old Punic, the language of the prayer books. He writes lines from a text he learnt as a child. He used to know it by heart, though he never knew what it meant. When he was little he used to chant it to himself when he lay in his bed, afraid of the darkness, and it was a comfort to him. He used to chant it silently inside himself without moving his lips. There was comfort in the secret sound of his own voice in the house of himself, in the house that lay in the dark room. He writes,

> *and the daughter of Hammon is left as a cottage in a vineyard, as a lodge in a garden of cucumbers, as a besieged city...*

That is all he thinks he remembers, yet his hand continues to write.

> *your country is desolate, your cities are burned with fire, strangers devour the land in your presence. It is overthrown by strangers...*

The sun has gone and the light in the room is dim magenta, crepuscular. His mother is lighting three little lamps on a stand. She speaks as if there had been no break in the conversation.

'And anyway, where would we move to?'

'We could go back to Tyre. You've still got family in Tyre.'

'Why would we want to go back to Tyre? It's such a distance. Weeks it would take. I was a girl when I first came to Carthage. A bride I was then. We were weeks and weeks on the sea.'

'A lot of people are moving away. They're frightened. There were Romans in the library today, a delegation. They were being given the tour. That Cato, the ex-Consul, he must be all of eighty, face like a pepper. He stopped right behind my desk. I was working on the minutes of some meeting. The old fellow went berserk. Accused the chief librarian of spying. The poor devil was trembling like a leaf.'

'Spying? What do you mean, spying?'

'He was just looking for trouble. That's why they're here. It was the same at the dockyard. Someone at the library told me he ordered them to stop work on the new slipways. The Romans are saying the city is planning to build a fleet of warships. Chap on the fruit stall said it's common knowledge in Rome that another war is being planned.'

His mother is rummaging in the shopping.

'What did you buy figs for? You know we never eat figs.'

8

With a flap and a crack the sail comes round and the *Osiris* heels into the crimson swells of unearthly morning, on the last long reach that will take her into the Gulf of Carthage. Spray breaks over the gunwale in dawn-lit rainbows. The ochre sail, a mote in all that lonely expanse of empty sea, glows orange in the light of the newly risen sun. She is an unlovely vessel, the *Osiris*, a round-bellied trader, built on a beach half a lifetime ago by pirates, and she wallows under the weight of her cargo, bales of flax, crates of sawn marble. Hanno stands by the steersman scanning the distant coast for the horned mountain and the pale smudge that is the city of Carthage, mother of oceans.

It is mid morning before the ship is threading the coastal sea-lanes. The inshore traffic is heavy, lateen sails flying downwind for Gabes oasis and the brickyards of Nabeul or beating northward for Utica. In the offing, a squadron of warships, fast Roman triremes.

The new dock wall is almost complete. It is more than a year since Hanno last made a landfall in his native city. The thing was scarcely begun when he left. The wall, built to protect the docks within, stretches like a fortress along the whole waterfront. Scaffolding still clings here and there to its towers. A forest of mast tops is visible above its rampart, all that can be seen of ships berthed in the inner harbour. The long expanses of new stone clang blank white in the sunlight. Against the harbour wall on the seaward side, rows of lighters from the quarries on the cape are moored six deep, jostling in the swell. The dockside is a mass of bullock carts, mule trains, porters, slave gangs.

Beyond the port rises the whaleback of the Byrsa, the citadel. It hangs shimmering in the rising heat of morning like a vision of the city of God, white colonnaded palaces, theatres, libraries, and the towers of the temples of Tanit, Melquart, Baal-Hammon. The lower slopes are a dim maze of steep streets. On the summit, catching the sunlight, the gilded rooftops of the Parliament.

This is the city of his birth, the lodestone that draws him with less and less insistence as the years pass. He was born in the district of Gapn in a tenement built on the ruins of Dido's palace. At least that was what he believed as a boy. You could see the stone bones of an ancient structure, arches and pillars, incorporated into the tenement wall. By the dye works there was a wall made up from fragments of ancient white marble, mouldings, cornices, cylindrical sections of fallen columns, stacked one upon another like something assembled by a child. The old tunnel-like streets of Gapn, between the Byrsa and the hill of Tanit, are a warren, an intricate maze. On the high ground beyond the cemeteries, the streets of the new town are straight and properly laid out.

In his mind's eye Hanno travels on beyond the district where he was born, across the lush suburbs of Megara, past the great triple city wall that looks out over the isthmus to broad miles of vineyards and farms, where goats stare in the black shade of olive trees and red water runs between date palms. Carthage's hinterland stretches a hundred miles inland to the frontier, to the fringes of the desert.

The desert is the mirage, the sign of oblivion, unimaginable. Wavering caravans emerge out of its wastes, undulating camel trains resolving out of the heat. Outward-bound caravans assemble in mud walled villages where towering dunes hang above the rooftops. Loaded camels, taller than the hovels, sway protesting through the narrow streets and the camel drivers curse and whistle. The long stately columns pass into the white silence, dwindling like the memory of dreams into the unthinkable emptiness.

In the stony, unkempt space between Carthage's city wall and the lagoon, close by the great sea gate, there is a fish market where the fishermen of the coast and the lagoon sell their catches from makeshift stalls, amid a confusion of drying nets, floats and fish baskets. The fishing boats are drawn up, chocked above the sand among stunted trees a hundred yards away on the lagoon beach. Packs of yellow dogs patrol the sand.

Spendios, the scribe is making his slow way from stall to stall with his mother on his arm, passing beneath tentacled banners of squid. The smell of fish is rich, undulating in the noon heat. His mother is looking for prawns and she is a woman of particular tastes. She prefers to buy her fish out here by the sea and will have no truck with the city fish markets. She prefers to buy her fish in the middle of the day when the fishermen are ready to go home. She drives a hard bargain. It is his day off from the library and Spendios is content to chaperone the fragile crone, holding a parasol over her head as she moves from stall to stall, tutting. Beyond, he can see ships passing into the harbour from the sea. White sails appear out of empty horizons. It is the mystery of the sea. He dreams, in his bachelor's narrow bed, of the sea, of endless oceans and the world's edge. He dreams with his eyes open through the paling of the morning star of white cliffs and blue men.

A big trading galley, *Phoenician*, out of Tyre or Sidon, moves majestically toward the sea gate, the harbour entrance, all gilded carving and sheer bulwarks, a floating city, an argosy. Behind her, dwarfed, her timbers bleached white, a Carthaginian trader returned from who knows which last, lost reach of ocean. He can just read her name in faded vermilion, *Osiris*: *Carthage*.

9

Hasdrubal is fat. The hot weather is a curse. Beneath the heavy brocade of his court tunic, sweat seeps along the folds of his powdered flesh. He is waiting for his litter to appear along the drive. From the wide balcony of his house in the suburbs of Megara he watches a slave pruning an ilex tree. The lawns of his house stretch down to the sea wall. He glimpses the cobalt glitter of the sea through lush fronds. The Gulf of Carthage is a taut blue horizon between the boles of palm trees. A slave girl crosses the lawn. It would engage his attention, this movement of black shining limbs against the green, this womanly motion, normally, but he is preoccupied. Normally he is a great fondler of slaves, a frequenter of brothels. He finds his silences among smooth limbs; in the slope of a hip, the curve of a belly and the shadowed depth of a navel. Today his mind is elsewhere.

He glances along the drive. It would not do to be late. He has been called to the Parliament. Called. There is no refusing. He

35

knows what is going to happen, in his politician's bones, with the prescience of his caste. His enemies have contrived it. It will seem like an honour, this appointment which they will offer him. He will be appointed as commander in chief of the new army of paid foreigners and raw recruits who are even now billeted in the villages up the coast. Rome has forbidden Carthage to raise an army. It is the central truth. During Hasdrubal's entire lifetime the interdiction has stood, since the defeat that Carthage suffered before he was born. Old Cato is here with his delegation and the Hundred have pleaded with him to be allowed to march against Numidia, and he has repeated the interdict, emphatically, unequivocally. Cato says he will intercede with the Numidians. It has been said before. It is a lie. The Numidian guerrilla bands grow bolder, more insolent by the year, pillaging estates that lie within a day's march of the capital. Refugees are a growing problem in the city. Revenues from outlying estates have been ruined.

When Hasdrubal takes this forbidden army and drives the Numidians back to their borders, Masinissa their king, ancient, wily Masinissa, will complain to Rome and Rome will declare war upon Carthage and Hasdrubal will be the scapegoat. Hasdrubal will lose whichever way the dice roll. If he defeats the Numidians, Rome will be enraged and Hasdrubal will be blamed. If he fails to defeat them, he will be blamed in Carthage for incompetence and cowardice.

Hasdrubal understands another truth, a truth known and not known, a truth never spoken, never spoken of, a truth known only by the silences and evasions which hedge it about. In the Parliament on the Byrsa, when the Hundred are howling at one another like dogs across the speaker's staff, this truth is a silence above the noise of the pack.

There is a dream. It comes to Hasdrubal like a revenant, comes and stands quietly beside him as he sleeps. It is the dream of that unsayable truth. In the dream, seabirds cry and the wind blows across the summit of a hill making a sound among the dry grasses. The ground is stony, broken, and the grass grows up between the stones. The stones are not desert stones worn smooth by the centuries. The stones are broken. It is ashlar, masonry, building stone, and it stretches across the level summit like a carpet as far as the eye can see beneath the hushing grasses. Not one stone stands upon another. Hasdrubal is absent from this place. In his dream he wonders why. He wonders where he is.

Across the lawns, in the blue-black shadow of the palms he can see his wife making her way toward the house. She is carrying the youngest in her arms, though there are slaves walking behind, and from the set of the child's body he can see that she is asleep. His son trails along holding on to the hems of his mother's skirt. For a moment the figures are etched blackly against the brilliant sea. Hasdrubal sees them, half sees them, through the mist of his preoccupations, and does not think about them at all. He is thinking about Rome. Rome hangs like a storm cloud along the horizon of his imagination.

She is victorious in Spain and Macedon. Her legions have enslaved the cities of Greece. Italy is her kitchen garden. She has no enemies left in the world, will suffer no enemies. The question that hangs in the Roman senate is the question of Carthage. Other questions have been answered, other nations brought to ruin. Rome is in Carthage now: red-faced Cato and his troop of sneering senators, a commission, a fact-finding tour. At the banquet he had been placed opposite to the old man. Cato had refused everything except bread and a few figs. He had looked Hasdrubal up and down as if he were a slave at an auction, a slave he had decided not to buy. He leant across to one of his fellow senators and said in loud Latin, 'Obesity comes of sloth.' Hasdrubal affected not to understand.

A gust of summer wind sweeps in from the sea and the palm tops plunge as if it were a storm. The little group crossing the lawn move in the hot blustery air like figures under the sea. The boy is hanging on to his mother's billowing hems. Her chiffon scarf flies away from her shoulders, up into the looping vortices of heat. The plunging palm fronds make a great soft clashing. The vermilion scarf swoops in the air, higher and higher.

The litter is waiting below him. Hasdrubal breathes in the welcome movement of air as he makes his way slowly down the white marble stairway. He feels the sweat running beneath his tunic. As he climbs into the canopied litter, his wife passes with their children across the clipped grass. For an instant their glances cross, like swords.

10

Yassib bangs his drink down.

'No, it's true. I've seen it. They crucify lions. They nail them up at crossroads. As God is my witness. They say that when lions grow too old to catch faster prey they begin to stalk people. They turn into man-eaters. The villagers organise hunts and when these old lions have been trapped and killed they nail the corpses up as a warning to other lions. As God is my witness. It's a strange thing to see, a crucified lion…'

More drinks arrive. Hanno is slightly drunk but at least he has stayed away from the card tables, which is just as well since he still has the crew's wages on him. Next to him, Yassib is more than slightly drunk. Yassib has only one eye and he wears an eye patch. They say he keeps a topaz behind the patch, in the empty socket. He is a shipper. He runs a lucrative business exporting wild animals to Rome. He also deals in dried chameleons and fake rhinoceros horn. He wears heavy gold bangles and a gold earring in the shape of a snake.

'…We ship a lot of lions these days. They kill them in Rome, dozens of 'em. Wild animal hunts are all the rage there… Lions against bears, bulls against packs of dogs. It's good business. Pays well, shipping animals. We ship all sorts. Crocodiles, we ship them direct from Egypt. We had a live rhinoceros in the warehouse last spring. We got it across all right in a big heavy-duty crate. We leased one of them big Tyrian galleys for the job, same as they use for elephants, but when they was unloading it at Ostia it broke out of its crate and fell into the river. Drowned it did. Not our responsibility I'm glad to say, once it was off the ship. Those Romans had paid top dollar too. The stevedores' guild had to foot the bill in the end. They wasn't happy. What I don't see is how they get them to fight each other. By the time those lions get to Carthage they're half dead, and that's before we've shipped them across to Italy. They sleep all the time, lions. You have to poke them to see if they're still alive.'

Hanno says,

'I've seen it.'

'What?'

'I've seen those animal hunts. We had a couple of days in Rome on the last trip. There were crate loads on the wharf, animals. The place was like a zoo. Ostriches. Wild dogs. Tigers.'

'Tigers! Wasn't none of our merchandise. We don't deal with the Far East. Too risky. It's two years before you get paid.'

Yassib is ruffled in his inebriation by the very thought of foreign competition but Hanno ignores him.

'There were two tigers in a crate. I watched them, these two tigers. Tigers have an interesting smell, by the way. Did you ever smell a tiger... no? Well anyway, they slept all the time, these tigers. Running they were, fidgeting and twitching in their sleep. Their paws were going as if they were running and their lips flicked back from their teeth every now and again. They were dreaming.'

'Animals dream? A misguided assumption. An antinomy.'

This is Taanach, a tallyman on the dock, a marker of cargoes, a conduit for bribes and backhanders, a lodestone for mercantile corruption, a philosopher. He says,

'Dreaming is an action of the soul. Animals have no soul. The ant, the bee, the grub: they have no soul. Women have no soul. Slaves have no soul. Menander, a pupil of Aristotle's, says that only men dream, because only men have a soul.

'Well, that's bollocks too. Whores dream.'

This is Yassib.

'I had this whore last night, big girl, black as jet, with that shiny skin and pink palms to her hands and pink insides to her cunt. Well, she fell asleep when it was all over. Snored, she did and her eyes were going under her eyelids and her fingers were working. Don't tell me she wasn't dreaming. She was like a little kid, you know, vulnerable, helpless somehow. Made me cry, it did.'

Yassib is very drunk. His eyes fill with sentimental tears. The memory of the sleeping whore makes him cry. Tears run down his cheeks. He says brokenly,

'If this Menander says that women have no souls, then he's a liar. Only a man who was afraid of women would write shit like that. Anyway he was a Greek, a shagger of boys. What did he know?'

Hanno does not speak. He is thinking of the stinking alleyway in the port of Rome, of the perfumed flesh in the darkness, of the falcon's cry. He lives in the recollection. It blooms unbidden, again and again. The memory races like a dolphin beneath a ship, a blue shadow rising out of the depths, vaulting out of the dazzling furrow that boils away from the bow's plough, turning in the light, faultless, unbearable, falling away again into the deep, into loss and the indigo roll of ocean.

He is a fool. Girls are girls, he tells himself. Spread thighs are spread thighs. It does him no good. He cannot bear the loss of the perfection of that trembling flesh, cannot bear the absence, cannot imagine having violated that blue veined beauty. He is a bear, a brute, a thing of gross and stinking appetite and yet it is *that* vision, of his grossness violating that fragility, which calls him, which will not be denied. He stands up. Cards, he will go and play cards. Yassib catches his sleeve.

'Oh no. Sit down, sailor, sit down. Sit. The siren call of the dice, is it? Of the cards? Sit down Hanno, brother, comrade, sweetheart. You must not gamble your ship away again.'

Yassib, not as drunk as he seems, is a better friend than Hanno deserves. He puts his arm across Hanno's shoulders and pulls the flagon across the table.

'Drink, drink. Here is a hogshead of angels.'

The following morning, Hanno is walking slowly in the shadow of a high wall. It is the wall that divides the docks from the city of Carthage. Shoeshine men and barbers ply their trade by the long wall. It is a vista of small time businesses. Here you can have your scalp massaged for a shekel, or your feet washed, or your horoscope cast, or your palm read, or the hairs plucked from your ears and nose. You can have a button sewn back on or a sandal repaired. Men stand about near the carts of tea wallahs, gossiping and drinking the hot sweet tea that is served from silver cups attached to the urn by chains.

Hanno has had himself shaved but his hangover is still poisonous. He walks in the shade. The bright sunlight is bad for his brain. He passes Spendios the scribe who is walking in the opposite direction on his way to his work at the library. Sometimes Spendios comes this way to buy a bagel for his lunch. There is a particular bakery just off the Agora which he favours. Today he will buy a slice of strudel to go with the bagel. The sailor and the scribe pass close to one another on the crowded pavement, almost touching, though their eyes do not meet. They do not even see one another and will never know that they have passed so close. Spendios saw Hanno's ship, the *Osiris* arriving two days ago when he was out by the harbour entrance with his mother shopping for fish, though he does not remember.

They will speak together one day, the scribe and the sailor, near the end, when the time is crowding in.

The scribe reaches the end of the high wall and comes out into the Agora. The day is fine and blue and still and there is warmth in the winter sunshine. In the shadows there is a rare skin of ice on the puddles. He stands outside the bakery eating the extra bagel he has bought. Down the side street slaves are sitting in the sun with their backs against the wall. They are white with flour after a shift in the back turning the big stone querns. Black slaves covered in white flour. They are eating bagels too and the bread steams in the air as they break it open. They joke with one another, showing white teeth.

The Agora is busy. Today is a feast of Tanit and people are passing in and out of the temple doors. Vendors are selling little votive images of the goddess at the bottom of the temple steps, little figures pressed from tin and copper and ersatz silver. Spendios sees a child move away from a vendor with its mother and father, clutching a little emblem. He sees the glint as it slips to the pavement. There is a flicker of family consternation. The little image has slipped between paving stones. The three crouch around the place where the lost object has disappeared. The father tries with his wife's hairpin to retrieve the little image from between the pumice slabs but it is no use. The child is inconsolable. She will have nothing to do with any of the other gewgaws that are for sale and is led away, tragically. Spendios pictures the lost image in its secret place and wonders who will ever find it. He walks over brushing bagel crumbs from his fingers and stands over the place of loss, above the cleft in the world where secrets are kept.

Hanno the sailor needs to find a particular shipping office. He is not quite sure where it is. Yesterday he did the rounds of the shipping agents with Mattho, the first mate, looking in a vague sort of way for a new contract for the *Osiris*. They drift through the maze of alleys where the shippers have their offices. Billions of talents worth of business pass through these dingy offices every year, yet the whole quarter is rundown and unkempt. Runners and tallymen lounge in doorways. Business is conducted above the street, up narrow wooden stairs by fat men with betel-stained teeth. Cargoes and destinations and prices are scrawled in chalk on blackboards on the narrow pavements. Mattho the mate had been, as he thought subtly, drawing Hanno's attention to jobs involving a landfall in Sidon.

'Look at this, Sidon, out and back. Slaves on the outward trip and cedar on the return. There and back, simple. We could stick out for a percentage. We could be back here before the autumn gales: a doddle.'

'I'm not doing any more slaves. I've told you that.'

'What about this then. Furniture to Sidon. Down the Lebanese coast to Tyre. Dyed cloth from Tyre to Carthage. Another piece of piss. We don't want to get stuck for the winter again in some godforsaken pirate town. I've got family here, you know, wife, kids. The kids hardly know me. The last one, Kankanaya, was walking before we got back from the last trip.'

'Kankanaya?'

'Worse than that. Her mother gave her a middle name too. Targuziza.'

'Kankanaya Targuziza?'

'Wasn't my idea. Nobody asked me, because I wasn't around to ask, was I? That's what happens if you stay away too long. Look. Look at that, at the top of the list. Canaan, that's the place. Tyre, Sidon, nice towns. There and back before the next one arrives.'

'You've got a woman in Sidon. I know why you want to go there. I'm going to save you from yourself. Look at this.'

'What?'

'Look there at the bottom.'

'Belerion? The Out Isles? That's even further North than Armorica. You can't go there. Anyway it's banned, you know that, anything beyond Ophuissa. Too much shipping lost out there. It goes on forever they say. The seas are higher than the mast top. What do you want to go there for? I heard that the sea goes thick like porridge in those latitudes.'

Hanno gives him a look.

'A lot of fog and ice anyway, same thing, and the men have their dicks tattooed blue.'

'And the women have big white thighs...'

'What?'

'Big thighs... the women... pale skin, blue veins, fair hair... and keen.'

'What? Where d'you hear that?'

'It's a well-known fact. Very keen.'

Mattho's face is clouded, but he resists the lure.

'Anyway you can't go there. It'd be a whole year. What about my family? The rest of the crew won't be too happy.'

'Look at the percentage on the job. You can get rich doing jobs like that.'

'You can get in a lot of trouble doing jobs like that.'

'I've never been to Belerion.'

'Neither have I, and there's a good reason for that.'

The two sailors come out at the dockside, into the bright sunlight and the din. The inner harbour, Cothon, the cup, as it is known, is three hundred yards across and it is solid with shipping. Vessels pass ceaselessly in and out of the dock gate that leads to the outer harbour and the sea. Above the forest of masts rises the harbourmaster's tower, its balconies patrolled by the dock police with loudhailers.

In the old days before the war, the inner harbour used to be an arsenal, a naval dockyard where warships were built and refitted, but in the peace that was imposed after the defeat at Zama, Carthage was forbidden to maintain a fleet of warships. The grand fleet had been towed out into the gulf and burned. The whole city had been ordered out to watch. The arsenal had stood empty for years, its massive lock gates closed, the great chains rusting, a bad luck place, the haunt of solitary eel fishermen, a silent symbol of defeat, humiliation, the wide stretch of water empty. A generation passed. Young men grew up who had never known the war. The rotting dock gates were reopened and merchant shipping began to use the slipway moorings. The sheds which once housed war galleys have become warehouses and markets. Round bellied merchant ships, hippoi, workhorses, are built in the sheds where once warships were drawn up. These days few but the very old choose to remember the war at all. Mostly it is the midwater trade that uses the inner harbour. Cargoes of olive oil go out from here to Sicily, Spain, the South of Italy, and cut stone, the florid pink veined marble that is quarried in the interior: pottery, textiles, slaves, wine, general cargoes. The big corn boats use the outer harbour, and the vast Lebanese and Egyptian galleys.

The two men stand at the dockside. They are at cross-purposes, frustrated with one another. Below them the water of the harbour, thick with refuse, slaps against slime-green masonry. Mattho kicks a fish head into the water.

'Anyway, I know why you want to go to the Out Isles. You want to get away from that aristocratic tart you shagged on the dockside. You've been like a bear with a sore head. Who do you think you are, Himilco the fucking explorer?'

'It's my ship. I'll go where the fuck I want.'

'You'll be needing another first mate then, won't you?'

Mattho leaves him standing there, at the water's edge. Out in the harbour two ships are fouled, their spars and rigging entangled. There is a booming of megaphones from the admiral's tower. The crews of the ships are gesticulating and shouting abuse at one another in their mutually incomprehensible languages. On the deck a bare and contemptuous arse is displayed, waggled.

11

Hasdrubal's wife stands behind the long gauze curtain looking out on the moonlit garden. A peacock calls from the darkness beyond the silvered lawns. The night is very still and hot and above the noise of cicadas she can hear distant wavelets lapping the shore. She is restless, hot and restless. She imagines walking down through the moonlit garden to the sea. She imagines her feet in the shallows, imagines the sand between her toes. She breathes in the blossom-scented air. She stretches out her arms wide in the darkness and feels the thin stuff of her nightgown move against her nipples.

Hasdrubal has gone. He has packed his crates of dress uniforms and gone. He has abandoned his unpaid tailors and gone to his war. All of the generals and the hangers-on who have infested the house these last days are gone too. She has closed the door of his study, closed the door on the wide desk avalanched with discarded maps, despatches and letters. She can make no picture of this war he has gone to, though half the young men in the city seem to have gone with him, even some of her own gardeners. Numidia is a neighbouring kingdom. There are Numidians living in Carthage. Her own brother is married to one of Masinissa's daughters. Hasdrubal's wife pictures the princess her brother's wife. She is tall and straight backed, with dense black crimped hair and a kind of hesitant beauty. When she is startled her head comes up, like a gazelle. Hasdrubal's wife is aware of her husband's absence as a feeling of relief. The house breathes more quietly. She prefers his absence. The children prefer it.

She dressed up the two children in their best for the formal leave taking and he picked them up and kissed them and he was crying, blubbering, copious tears that made the whole creased slab of his face wet and foolish. And he kissed her too, clung to her, pressing his great wet face into her neck.

After all the years she does not know what to make of him: a man, the enemy, a tyrant, a dangerous and frightening child, but less and more than that. She knows about his whores, about the slave girls. His lasciviousness, his unfocussed lust comes off him like heat. He would fuck a baboon, a pig, a keyhole, his wife thinks. He has to do it. He has to do it to her too. He looms over her, crushes her beneath the clumsy, sweating mountain of his body and somewhere within the fortress of her resistance she reaches out to him, though he leaves her bruised and empty like the dry skeleton of a boat on a beach. Her desire is all lack, loss, absence. She craves fragrance, subtle insistence, the arched passivity of ecstasy.

She unfastens her nightgown and lets it fall to the floor. She stands naked in the darkness running her own hands over her body, waiting for the lift of the latch and the sound of bare feet across the floor.

12

'You're not going, and that's that.'

The mate's wife is standing in the doorway of the house, her big belly blocking his way. Mattho is standing in the narrow hallway with his kit bag.

'You said. "Sod him," you said, "I'm not going," you said. Well you're not. What about the kids? What about me?'

Little Kankanaya is clinging on to Mattho's leg, bawling.

'It's the last time, I swear. Hanno says this one will make us rich, and anyway we'll be back in three months.'

'That's not what you said. "At least a year." That's what you said. "That's why I'm not going," you said. "I want to be here when the next one's born," you said.'

Mattho picks up the tiny girl and she clings to his neck, still yelling. Waves of panic rise up in him.

'No, look...'

'No. You look.'

He is trapped, a prisoner in his own hallway. It is noon. The *Osiris* is due to leave her berth at noon. In his mind's eye he sees the ship slipping her moorings and moving away down the harbour toward the open sea. The impulse to escape overwhelms him. He disentangles the little girl from his neck and pushes her into his wife's arms. Little Kankanaya fastens herself around her mother's neck.

'I'm sorry. I'm a shit. I can't help it.'

He moves his wife aside with a firm businesslike movement and squeezes past. She is holding the child and can do nothing to stop him. In a moment of outrageous affection he kisses her on the cheek as he passes and then he is out, gone, running down his street, stumbling over his kit bag, fleeing the shrill abuse, running the gauntlet of scandalised shutters.

He comes out between warehouses breathless at the dockside. The *Osiris* has gone. A Sicilian oiler is manoeuvring into the vacant berth. He begins to run again, down the length of the outer dock, looking this way and that as he runs, for the ship among the jostling masts. He trips over a hawser and goes down painfully on the stones. His kit bag skids away from him and disappears over the edge of the dock.

'Shit, shit, shit.'

He hobbles on, wincing and bobbing. He is coming toward the harbour entrance and he catches the distant dazzle of the sea and still he cannot see the *Osiris* among the confusion of masts.

He stops, his breath sobbing hopelessly in and out. He imagines the ship out there, heeling into the blue water, heading for the horizon, and his eyes fill with impotent tears. A castaway: no ship, no home.

The harbour mouth is solid with shipping, a moving forest. Two, three vessels out he catches a helmsman's profile against the light.

Mattho has jumped onto the deck of the galley moored against the dock and gone down on his sprained foot with a yell. He goes crabwise across the deck and launches himself from the gunwale. He clings for a moment over the water to the slowly passing barge, his fingers uncurling as he struggles for a foothold, and swings aboard. He scrabbles up the piled cargo of melons and dozens of the huge fruits cascade away from him and over the side. He is aware of running feet, hostile voices. From the summit of the melon mountain he sees Hanno a few yards off, moving past at the helm of the *Osiris*, his eye on the harbour mouth. Mattho is sitting on the mountain of melons shouting in inaudible rage across the din of shipping as the two vessels pass only yards apart. He starts to slide down the other side of the melons and this time the whole long slope of piled fruit is on the move. Mattho goes over the side in a yellow avalanche.

Hanno looks down from his place at the steering oar of the *Osiris* at the mate spluttering among a hundred bobbing melons.

'You're late.'

On the unkempt beach by the harbour mouth the fishermen are selling their catches. It is Spendios' day off again and he is

47

escorting his mother as she moves with a critical eye from one stall to the next. Today she is looking for squid. The scribe moves at her elbow, patiently. Behind him the *Osiris* passes out through the sea gate and turns toward the horizon.

The Desert

13

The army of Carthage begins to move, gathering itself to itself. Battalions of infantry form up at the edges of villages where they have been billeted and join the slow tide of marching columns. Baggage wagons move in a swelling convoy at the rear with a great noise of wheels over stony ground. Whores walk arm in arm behind the bullock carts, among the packmen and the beggars.

In the evening, crossing the tepid mile-wide shallows of the delta, flamingos rise up in wheeling, livid pink clouds, turning across the hugely setting sun. At night the campfires flicker everywhere in the level darkness. Recruits examine their blistered feet and wonder why they are here. Sounds come from far off: the sound of tethered horses: distant laughter.

By noon of the second day the host is traversing a plain of salt-rimed sand. A great flag of dust a hundred feet high and a mile across drifts away from the moving columns. In the immensity of the salt flats the army moves microbially. There are stretches where the sand is littered with salt crystals, horizon to horizon. The declining sun sets them aflame and for a few moments the entire plain burns crimson.

On the fourth day riders come in out of the filmy wastes, spies. They walk their dust-white horses beside Hasdrubal's litter. He raises the awning a little. The Numidians are a day ahead, a little off the Carthaginian line of march. Horsemen, many horsemen, shrouded Tuaregs from the interior, driving herds of camels and goats and captives. Hasdrubal waves his spies away and they drop back through the trudging columns of infantry. He lets the awning fall and sinks into the cushioned twilight of the litter.

On the sixth day groups of Numidian riders canter out of the parched levels and run the gauntlet of the marching columns at a gallop, crying like peacocks, their faces hidden within billowing burnooses. Lines of dust rise behind them, hang in the air like a memory of their passing. Through the day they appear out of the heat shimmer, gallop the length of the army and veer away again with shrill ululating cries, melting back into the wavering heat, until their appearance raises no gust of apprehension among the stolid files of men and boys. The youths in the newly raised levies, the marching ranks of boys who last week were apprentices, gardeners, labourers and thieves in the city, call out, jeering and clowning. They are tickled by their own wit.

Towards evening the horsemen emerge through the mirages again, more of them this time, galloping as before along the length of the marching columns. It is a show and the boys are jeering and calling out to them. Someone throws a coin. Suddenly they have turned in toward the columns and are coming in at a dead run, arrows already nocked. The Carthaginian column ripples and the arrows go in like hornets. The veiled riders are almost into the mass of infantry before they turn, dragging their mounts round viciously only feet from the jostling panic stricken recruits, the scuttering hooves spraying sand and stones. The moment is full of red dust and noise and terror. Inexplicably, a screaming infantryman is dragged away by the heel trailing a cone of dust behind the retreating horsemen. There are a dozen dead from the attack and twice that number wounded. Young soldiers are shouting and milling about and the foreign NCOs are laying about with their batons, pushing the panicky recruits back into their ranks and cursing. A boy who has been shot twice, through the face and through the neck, is sitting upright with the arrows still in him, waiting for a surgeon. He sits slightly apart from his comrades in the space his bad luck has created for him.

That night the Carthaginians build no fires. Pickets are doubled. The sound of the screaming infantryman comes loud through the silent darkness. The boys in the levies, only a week from home, are crying into their blankets for their mothers. The next day, outriders are posted along the flanks of the army.

On the eighth morning low cloudbanks can be seen hanging on the horizon and by evening this cloud has resolved into pale dun coloured upland. The long columns pass into the dim hills. It is a broken country stretching featureless to every vague horizon, where colours are reduced to shades of ash and salt blue. Here and there outriders cross the hint of a track or the white bone litter of a forgotten slave route. Two camels moving distantly among thorns draw the eye. A village, a tiny cubist smudge in the huge space takes half a day to crawl across the horizon. The smokes of its small destruction shimmer against the blue grey. The army falls into a kind of trance. In the stifling half-dark of his litter Hasdrubal slips in and out of dreams.

Spies come in and go out again. The Numidian army is a mirage, melting away before the crawling columns of the army of Carthage. Dust-white riders canter out of the looping phantasmal horizon and walk alongside Hasdrubal's litter like death's men. From within the lurching litter he listens to their reports and he feels that he is advancing against nothing, against a chimera, a dream, a phantom horde of shrouded horsemen. There is no city, no centre. He is advancing upon a vanishing empire of tents and swirling tribesmen. He burns a village here and there, slaughters a few unwary nomads: small shards of reality in the dreamlike void. With every mile he feels the supply lines stretching to nothing behind him. Carthage wishes to forget him, is forgetting him already, as it forgot Hannibal fifty years ago, by an act of will. For twelve years Hannibal and his army wandered Italy like unhoused avenging ghosts, and now, in the city of Carthage the army of Hasdrubal is just another half-forgotten story.

Somewhere out in the windblown sand of the desert is Masinissa, the king. Years ago Hasdrubal met him. Masinissa could sit a whole day without moving, like a lizard or a snake, and at the end of long hours he would rise from his throne without effort, poised and dangerous. Hasdrubal's veiled intuition is that finally the Numidian king will turn and offer battle, because the old man is proud and would not be content to be thought an insubstantial and cowardly spirit of the desert.

On the tenth day, comes a stroke of luck, for good or ill. Outriders canter in, escorting a troop of Numidian cavalry under the sign of parley. It is two of Masinissa's lieutenants. There has been a quarrel among the Numidian kinglets. Masinissa has three legitimate grown sons and an uncertain number of bastards. The lieutenants, Anasis and Stuba, two of his bastards, sit their horses impassively as the nervous interpreter delivers the message. They offer six thousand cavalry, who are camped over the horizon, to Carthage. They seek to avenge themselves upon the basilisk king and his faithless sons. It is a matter of honour, says the interpreter, repeatedly. The young men are also seeking the throne of the kingdom of Numidia, though they are too polite to mention the matter. Hasdrubal looks at these two black handsome young aristocrats, clinking with martial accoutrements, stiff-necked with haughty punctilio, and he knows they are dead men. He accepts their offer. Against the vast disc of the setting sun the deserting cavalry squadrons swing inward across the levels at a gallop, black and wild in the red light.

Hasdrubal writes a letter to Masinissa to make sure the old king is aware of this turn of events. He writes the letter that is calculated to bring the old cobra to a stand. In it, he laments the old man's divided kingdom. He sympathises with him. Turbulent sons are a curse, impossible to bring to heel, when one has grown old... and feeble. Would the old man like to make terms? It is not a letter he would wish to deliver in person.

Among the spies is a rider whose name is Qart, a scholar once they say, a novice in the priesthood, a chess player, subtle in dispute, civil and reserved in his speech, but mad, a killer, a cannibal. Hasdrubal sends for him. 'I want you to take this letter to Masinissa.' Qart guesses what is in the letter and knows that to deliver it may well prove a death sentence. Hasdrubal knows he knows. He also knows that Qart is a man of his word: more than that, a man who is his word. Said is done. He is irresistible in his self-hatred and he asks more money for the job than he thinks Hasdrubal is willing to pay. Without demur the fat man agrees to the price. Qart stands in the sumptuous tent that is a scandal in its opulence for an army on the march, white with dust from head to foot, his red-rimmed eyes unblinking. He takes the letter from Hasdrubal's hand and the money. He takes two horses and more water and food than the journey requires. He leaves the encamped army in darkness, passing through the pickets, calling out the day's passwords as he goes. When the outposts are behind him he urges the horses forward, canters out toward the unseen horizon, between the black and the black. It is where he has to be; outside, beyond.

Masinissa is eighty-eight. He is sitting outside his tent watching the sun set. Beneath the heavy lids the eyes are yellow and rheumy with age, but his back is straight. He sits as if he were carved from stone. His latest child, a girl, two years old, is playing at his feet. King Masinissa is a legend, and it makes him tired.

The letter is in his lap. Ten years ago he would have killed this messenger, sent him home, dismembered, in a sack. It is what is expected of him. He looks up slowly at the rider. This one would prefer to be dead, and besides, it is of no importance. It is a game, all of it. It is something that occurs to him more often these days. None of it matters: not the death of this messenger: not the battle he is about to initiate. He is surrounded by his sons, young bulls who jostle and push and know nothing. They want to eat the world, these young men. In the cosmic tree there are two birds. One eats. The other watches it eat. Masinissa does not eat. In his eighty eighth year, he watches. He knows too much to eat. These days he pretends to eat. He prefers the company of women. He does what has to be done, what is expected. He knows he will have to turn and face this Carthaginian and his army of conscripts and hired foreigners, this fat man, this Hasdrubal the Boetharch, whose reputation for deviousness and self-seeking stinks even in the cesspit that is Carthage. This Hasdrubal must think him a very stupid man if he thinks he will rise to such sneering bait as this. The fat man must know that he was always going to turn and offer battle to his enemy. He wanted only to draw him far enough into the desolation that is his kingdom, his inheritance, to entice him far enough from Carthage, from food, water, from all hope of rescue.

Masinissa pictures the two sons who have deserted him and guesses at their agony of mind. He pictures their cavalry squadrons, encamped like lepers a little distance from the Carthaginians. Deserters have two choices, prevail or die. Tomorrow he will start a battle in which his own sons will fight on opposite sides. The thought makes him tired, but they expect it. They expect ruthlessness, his unruly princes, so he will give them ruthlessness. He is the puppet of his legend. At some point, which he cannot quite remember, he fell under the shadow of his own fame and lost the power to choose.

His eyes have never left the thin white rider. He says in his own tongue,

'Do you play chess?'

The head inclines.

'Good. I like to play chess on the eve of a battle. It puts things in perspective, a game of chess.'

He sighs and after a moment he leans down and picks his tiny daughter up.

'What do you think? Pretty, is she not, like her mother.'

Daybreak. The Numidian banners drift in the wind. The battle line is a mile long, a filament of horses and men and flags along the saffron skyline. The columns of Carthage come slowly to a halt as the troops in the leading battalions become aware of the distant enemy. There has been no order, no trumpet call. The army simply comes to a halt. Hasdrubal knows immediately and orders his litter bearers forward. He comes out beyond the leading standards and gets out of his ridiculous ruched satin palanquin with difficulty, stands on the desert in his embroidered slippers, squinting into the dusty wind, a fat man in a wide stony space between armies. His eyes move along the distant battle line. He can pick out infantry formations in the centre but overwhelmingly it is an army of horsemen. On either wing cavalry regiments stretch to the edge of sight, so many of them. Their pennants and banners are a forest. He cannot hope to hold a battle line with his army of untrained infantrymen. He must allow these swirling tribesmen to envelope him. He has no choice. Let them wear themselves out with their whooping charges. They will not penetrate the pikes. He will set his phalanxes in an open square. If his Carthaginian boys, his costermongers, his apprentices and barrow boys will stand, if they will simply stand up straight and hold on to their pikes and not call out to their mothers and not run away, if his motley battalions of pimps and cobblers will simply stand in the lines he puts them in then they will mostly survive.

The mercenaries, Spaniards, Celtiberians, Gauls, will do what they have to and no more. They will stand because of what they know. To run is to die, and besides, there is some code among the hired regiments, some ragged principle that lifts them a little above the common run of criminals. Most of the officers are sound; professionals, tradesmen. The honour of the paid soldier lies in standing his ground. He serves who stands, who stands the ground, any ground, the chosen ground. His is the body, the weapon, the numb cudgel of blood and bone. For the rest, the hired soldier is a brute, a thief, a raper of women, an arsonist. Hasdrubal will set his regiments of boys between the foreigners where he can.

He does not know about his Numidian deserters. Their hope can only be in victory for the army of Carthage, yet he has no sense of their mind. He cannot read these black princes who command them. At the back of all his thinking Hasdrubal knows he has been drawn into a trap. If they lose the day, if the army fragments in panic then they will all die, all of them. They have been drawn too far into this forsaken desolation to have any hope of escape. The Numidian butchers will harry them, hack them down, and amuse themselves in their encampments with the survivors through the night. Today Carthage must stand its ground, no more. Today he will teach his barrow boys to do that at least. He calls up the commanders.

The dawn wind drives the dust that is raised by the evolutions of the battalions, so that the army of Carthage moves in a miasma, a bright fog of dust. The sun is still below the horizon but the sky is darkly radiant. The army prepares for battle in a thickening golden obscurity. Shouted orders, the sound of whistles, drums, horses, can be heard in this dim dream. The recruits are mute atoms in this universal organism, their minds blank, as they march and counter march. Spectral columns emerge and fade, evolving into long ranks, four deep, into phalanxes. The wavering lines are dressed, fingertip to shoulder, fingertip to shoulder, receding into the golden fog. The heavy pikes are issued from open carts that pass between the ranks. The pikes come up like fields of corn, numberless against the risen sun.

Donkeys laden with panniers of lead slingshot pass along the lines of naked slingmen as they are applying paint to their bodies. They heft the shot and grimace at one another. Inferior stuff, moulded by idiots. The sling men abuse the muleteers as they pass down the line, in a language which sounds to the transport men like the speech of animals.

Boxes of arrows are broken out from the lashed down carts and issued to the companies of Spanish archers. They squint along the shafts, turning them for their truth and push them into the streaming sand at their feet in rows.

They have played through the night, Masinissa and the spy, beneath plunging torches. The shadows of the pieces waver in the uncertain light, lengthening and shrinking away. The old man watches as the spy sits motionless with his finger on the top of his queen and then makes the move that seals his fate. The king says,

'Does it not make you afraid, winning these games? A man might feel it prudent to lose once in a while.'

'I rest in the king's wisdom, in his generosity of spirit. I would not insult him.'

The accent is formal, old fashioned, as if he had learned the language from his grandfather, or from a book. The old man knows he is being mocked.

'You are nothing to me. A spy, flotsam, nothing. I could smear you like an insect.'

Qart says nothing, letting him sit in the unbecoming echo of his own utterance, letting it hang in the air, rebuking him. The king, unthinkingly, unthinkably, accepts his rebuke, owns it. Troubling humility expands within him in fans and circles like water spreading across a floor. It is as if this thin dusty man were his angel, come to instruct him in the last things. The old man pushes his king over, and says,

'A king does not need to be wise. He only needs to be strong.'

The spy is looking at the prone piece, the surrendered game.

'Brutes are strong. A king sees more than other men. Is it not so?'

Mockery flickers, lightning on the horizon. The impulse rises again in the old man to rid himself of this irritant, to flick it away. The habit of power rises in him like a crocodile, fatal and unknowable, then sinks away again, and he smiles inwardly despite himself. He must sit a little longer with this teacher of the heart. He begins to reset the pieces.

'Another game?'

He looks up beneath his heavy lids and catches his opponent's gaze. The skin around the eyes creases for a moment and a faint polar smile passes like a ghost across the spy's features. The old man frowns in the glare of its beatitude.

'Another game.'

Sometime in the middle of the night when they are still far from the shores of morning, Masinissa begins to speak.

'When I was a young man, Hannibal the Carthaginian was in Italy with his army and the Romans could not drive him out. They had no general to match him. The war seemed to be everywhere in those days. There was fighting in Italy, Spain, Sicily, even on the seas. At last the Romans carried the war into Africa. They voted in the Senate to do it. They are a remarkable people. They sent that Scipio who was later called Africanus with an army across the sea to Africa to lure away the allies of Carthage and to threaten the city itself. In the end Hannibal had to leave Italy and return with his army to defend his native city, as the Romans had hoped, and he was defeated in a great battle out in the salt desert at a place called Zama, and Carthage was defeated.'

Masinissa sits for a moment in recollection. He pushes back the sleeve of his tunic and raises his forearm. On the underside like a pale road on an ancient map a scar runs from wrist to elbow.

'This is my memento of that battle, my keepsake. It whispers to me when the weather is damp. But that was all later. In the time I am speaking of Hannibal was still spreading terror in Italy, and Scipio had yet to come to Africa and fight his war of ruin against the city of Carthage.

At that time Numidia was an ally of Carthage. My father was king in Numidia and I was away in Spain with the cavalry fighting with the Carthaginians against the Romans. Word came to me that my father had died and the kingdom had been betrayed into the hands of Syphax, a neighbouring king.

I came back from Spain to my own country with a few of my young men and began raising troops in the villages and towns where I knew that support for my family's cause could be found. It was all foolishness, but then I was a young man. Death or Glory. I would reclaim my father's throne or die in the attempt.

The village boys would steal the farm horses and their fathers' rusty swords and ride after me. I became a kind of brigand. We ambushed Syphax's patrols, attacked isolated outposts, made a nuisance of ourselves. We had some success and I had a name in the country but there was no money, no organisation.

And then Scipio arrived with four legions, come to carry the war into Carthage's territory and draw Hannibal out of Italy to defend his own country.

For me it was fate's gift. I offered myself and my squadrons of village boys to Scipio. Syphax was the ally of Carthage and thus an enemy of Rome. For me, if I became an ally of Rome, there was a chance of reclaiming my father's throne. And of course I was a useful instrument for them, a young pretender to the Numidian throne with a following in the country.

In the days after my defection to Rome's cause it was Laelius, Scipio's lieutenant, who managed me. I can admire him now. He had a gambler's calm, an ability to look you in the eye and lie. He exploited my reputation for recklessness. He made of me a kind of, what would you say, a folk hero. My bravery was a legend. Now do not misunderstand me, spy, I am not more of a coward than the next man but Laelius turned me into a hero. It was his... what is the word... his policy, this fiction: a national hero fighting alongside the liberating army of Rome to throw off the Carthaginian yoke. Laelius showered me with gifts, praised my godlike bravery and I, being young, believed it all. I can see his face now, his serious face. I never saw his laughter.'

'The Romans are a strange people. They venerate moderation. There is no passion in them and yet they are not to be turned aside. Their troops are like stolid peasants, like farmers, like blocks of wood. They have rules instead of passion. Even their cruelty is a practical thing. They destroyed Numidia and the provinces of Carthage with a kind of methodical calm. I have seen crops burning from horizon to horizon, towns and villages sacked where there was no garrison, no resistance, because it was their... their policy, while I fought my blind and foolish young man's war and to me life was all dash, reputation, vanity.

They marched them out of the towns and villages, everybody, the old, women, children, and killed them, calmly, like farmers cutting corn. Sometimes they would herd them into a barn and burn them. The name of Rome was Terror. They created a wasteland and called it peace.

And they will come again. Nothing is more certain. And this time they will farm the city of Carthage itself. They will gather in its crop of souls. There will be no treaty the next time, no armistice, no agreement, just a harvesting of souls, and if I am lucky I will not live to see it. They carry a disease with them, the Romans, and it has no name. They bring emptiness. The plague they carry is the void.'

The old man turns again to the game but it is no more than a gesture. The past demands utterance. He sits motionless in silence for minutes together then begins to speak again.

'In the months of that war I lived in the saddle. I was more horse than man. We rode and fought and rode again. I was half mad, in love with death, in love with myself. It is the way with young men. And behind me was Laelius like a puppet master, a whoremaster. I see it now. He ran me as a pimp runs a whore. I was Rome's whore.

And then it was over. We had the victory. The armies of Syphax had ceased to exist and Syphax himself had been captured. There he was in chains and stinking. When I rode toward him he stood up though he was loaded with chains and his ankles and wrists were bleeding cruelly. He was a man, Syphax. He knew me and I could have ridden him down, but he was not afraid, this man who had taken my father's city of Cirta for his own.

I said to Laelius, to my Roman whoremaster, 'Let me take this Syphax to Cirta, to that city whose gates are still shut against us, and show this person in chains to the citizens and they will certainly open the city gates to me, who am their rightful king.' And Laelius let me do it.

I was all pride and vainglory as I rode up to the gates of Cirta and revealed myself as my father's heir and demanded to be admitted to the city, but they jeered and whistled from the city wall and would not listen. I had Syphax brought to me and he limped out into that space before the city gates and he was far gone in pain and hunger. He stood there without shame, as a man, nothing else. I know now that he had learned much. In his adversity he had become... great is not the word... simple, is that the word, revealed to himself as what he was, so that he could stand there without either shame or pride. I did not know enough on that day to admire him. I admire him now. On the walls of Cirta they fell silent.

The city elders looked down at Syphax in his chains and they knew that the game was ended and they opened the gates. I clattered through like God himself into the city and up the cobbled streets to the palace with all my foolish heroes at my back.'

'Syphax had a wife. Her name was Sophonisba, a Carthaginian princess. It was a common joke among the armies in that war that Sophonisba was too much for Syphax, that her appetites were too great for him. They were poor jokes, soldiers' jokes. When I saw her standing among her women with her dark eyes and her heavy breasts I knew that it was true and that he had been through the fire with her. I also knew that even in his chains he still burned in that furnace.

It is difficult to speak of these things after so many years, difficult to speak of them at all. She was rare in her beauty, like an image in a temple but rich and ripe and alive. Desire rose up in me like fear and I knew Syphax then as a brother. She was dressed as if for a festival or a wedding, all jewels and feathers and shining skin and it flattered my foolish vanity. She threw herself about my knees. I can still see myself in that small bright space beyond the tunnel of the years, in all my young man's foolishness with that rare woman clasping my thighs. The gilded eyelids and the parted lips hang like a vision of the Goddess behind my old man's dreams.

She clung to my knees and she said that she was a princess of Carthage and that she would rather die than fall into the hands of Romans. I must give her freedom or give her death. I lifted her up and I had her then in front of that crowd, against a pillar and she was noisy in her transports. And I can say this to you, spy, because you are nothing to me. This was not the rapine of conquest. It was a thing of religion, a sort of worship. Homage. I lifted up the jewelled skirt and had the Goddess, had the darkness. Something else. It is the darkness that men desire and the little death, the rest that is to be found in that darkness. When I see a women jewelled and painted I see the idol, the goddess that men desire.

When Laelius arrived with his infantry the next day I had already married Sophonisba, the wife of Syphax. I had summoned priests in the night. If she was the wife of Masinissa the king then they could not make her a slave and carry her off with Syphax in chains to Rome, they could not defile her body. We had convinced

61

ourselves of this, she and I, in the make-believe spaces between our lovemaking.

Laelius was angry. I had never seen his anger before. I saw it then. He had managed me through that war, managed my youth, my impetuosity, my vanity and at last he had made a mistake. He had trusted me too far. He raged into the room where we lay, Sophonisba and I, and pulled away the covers so that we lay naked and ridiculous and he drew his sword and raged at me and chopped at the bedpost as if he would kill me.

I was cowed, humiliated, and I came to heel like a dog, a whore. When Scipio came later and listened to what had passed, he said to me that though she had asked me for her freedom it was not in my gift to grant it. 'She is Rome's prisoner before she is your wife. You must give her up. Besides, she is Syphax' wife before she is your wife. You must give her up.'

The dream was over. I woke to harsh necessity. I could not go against Scipio if I wanted to keep the city of Cirta, if I wanted to be king. I grew mad in my humiliation and in my impotence and my madness I reasoned thus: she has asked for freedom or death. I cannot grant her the first so I must offer her the second. These are memories that I flinch away from still, even after a lifetime, that I cannot look at with my head up.

I sent her a cup of poison. I sent it with a slave and a written message. I had not even the courage to go myself. The letter was conjured out of self-serving lies. Since I could not offer her freedom, I wrote, then I was bound by my word to offer her death. But I will swear to you, my teacher of the heart, that in my madness I did not even see that there was a choice to be made. I was a blind man. I must believe this in order to live.

The slave said that she read the letter and put it down again and after a moment she took up the poisoned cup and drank it down as if it were a glass of water and replaced it on the salver by the letter and turned away.

And all that dark beauty was invaded and lost. I saw her, still and stiff, with all the darkness fled and all the opulent heat and beauty grown cold. In my old man's dreams she rises up again. She rises like the moon. I am nothing to her yet she comes to me in her living darkness and I offer her the thin and bitter poison.

The slave said that there was no rebuke in her gestures. It was as if my betrayal of her were an ordinary thing, an expected thing. And it is an ordinary thing. We do it to them over and over. They come to us offering life and darkness and we betray them. We betray them to death. It is a dance. They come to the dance bearing life and we come bearing death and if it was intended thus then I am a madman.

When Scipio spoke to me afterwards he said that there had been no need for this tragedy. He spoke the truth. He would not have allowed her to come to harm.'

Masinissa falls silent and sits as if he were carved from stone. After an unmeasured silence he says,

'I took the throne. No. I was given the throne. My whore's reward. And I have been king now for a lifetime.'

Another silence, and then he speaks again.

'One thing. And here is the mystery. It is possible that all of the things she did, her marriage to Syphax, her marriage to me, her death, were all for a reason: and the reason that Sophonisba did these things was that she was a patriot. She did it all for the love of her native city Carthage.'

It is cold in the tent. Nothing moves except the shadows cast by the torch light. Outside, the dawn begins to create itself out of darkness. The sound is heard of distant hooves galloping. The captains are beginning to gather, the warriors. The old man raises his head at the sound.

'Listen, out there, all those young men baying for death, belling like hounds for the quarry.'

The dawn wind sends the valance of Masinissa's tent rattling. He listens to the sound of hooves and shouting outside the tent where impatient princes and staff officers sit their horses. The king's sons, his heirs and his bastards, mill about outside the tent on their glossy stallions. There is much rearing among the horses, much pawing of hooves and high stepping, and the princelings on their backs, all oiled ringlets, plumes, pennants and jewelled weapons, shout and gesticulate. Bodyguards and ostlers run about or hold on to bridles. The haughty princes are playing the part of haughty princes and the bodyguards and ostlers the parts of bodyguards and ostlers. It is a pageant, a simulacrum, an acting out of the real. The princes are waiting on their stamping, curvetting warhorses for the king to emerge and lead them through the mirror.

Inside the tent the king has conceded the game. He moves away from the board. His armour, arranged on its skeletal wooden mannequin is a spectre, a golem, in the thick light. He lifts the feathered fronds of his plumed helmet, runs his fingers across the gilt inlay of the cuirass. There was a time when all of this had meaning for him, when courage was a grail and battle a defining truth, when he too ran like a dog on the scent. The quarry is long gone, the scent grown cold. He withdraws the sword from its scabbard. The light is fluid along the chased steel, running like water as he turns the blade. Now he is doing what he must. He is the totem. He puts on the helmet and a cloak, leaving the sword and cuirass behind, and goes out.

There is a great shout, a great clashing of spears and rearing of horses. His own horse, held at the head, caparisoned, huge, stamps and sidles. The king puts his foot into the ostler's laced palms and swings up into the saddle, gathers the reins, looks about him for a moment at all the foolish, vainglorious panoply of battle, and is away, pounding and scattering the stones of the desert, with a confusion of princelings jostling in his wake. He stands up in the stirrups and makes the passage of the battle line at a gallop. He is a meteor and as he passes, the host dissolves forward with a roar, squadron after squadron in a long toppling wave, a thundering tide.

A mile away the Carthaginian barrow boys are moaning as they grip the heavy pikes. Piss runs down their legs as the ground begins to tremble. Silent archers and sling men take up positions between the pikes.

Hasdrubal is standing in the long thicket of steel, moving along the front rank that faces the approaching enemy, lifting the pikes to pass beneath as if he were wandering among apple boughs. He is singing and walking in the garden. He sings nursery rhymes and lullabies and speaks to his children by name. He is making a little summertime for them as he strolls among the heavy apple boughs, making a quiet place for them under the sound of the storm, beneath the gathering thunder that thrums in the chest and rocks the air. Hasdrubal has turned to face the enemy. He stretches out his arms among the pikes, the long steel blades passing either side of his body and above his head. He is singing louder now, a deep and steady baritone. His battle hymn is a street song, known to everyone, full of vulgarity and innuendo, but he sings it slowly as if he were in the temple. Ridiculous and terrible, fat, weaponless, in his slippers, he is holding his wavering thousands with his outstretched fingertips and the sound of his voice, the idea of his voice. At last his choir begins to take up his stately brothel tune, begin in ones and twos to sing the words. The sound grows, ebbs, grows again, goes out along the panicking ranks. They are singing as the pikes are braced, out of the void of their terror and the sound they make is the deep sound of the ocean surf. It rolls along the line end to end in great slow waves, rising and falling, profound, outside of the world: a hymn to the time.

14

Spendios looks up from his journal for a moment. His shadow sits in the square of sunlight on the wall, the balding wisps of his hair precisely silhouetted by the level light.

This morning mother insisted I deliver a package to our neighbour Mara, lace bobbins, some unnecessary nonsense. My mother contrives to send me to the houses of women she thinks are eligible. It is her game. Our game. We both pretend that I am an eligible bachelor. We have been playing our game for years now. Mara is a widow. She works at the laundry, a square faced, strong looking woman. Her son is with the army of Hasdrubal in Numidia. There is no news yet of the expedition. He is all she has and she worries. A tall, ungainly boy, not attractive at all, but then I'm not his mother. She tried to dissuade him from enlisting and they quarrelled. The boy left in a rage. I believe he struck her, though she did not say as much. She worries in case he doesn't come back, in case they never make amends. Of course he'll be back I say. It will all be over in a few weeks. He'll be back, you'll see.

15

Qart hands Hasdrubal the package from Masinissa. The fat man is sitting in his litter with the curtains thrown up over the canopy to let in the air. The ornate palanquin sags ruinously, its gilded frame leaning to one side, its pleated drapery torn and white with dust. The stench of pestilence hangs in the unmoving air, a smell of latrines and unburied dead. The ground is too hard to bury those who have died. They lie stinking under piles of stones and the sound of flies is loud. The hilltop camp is a vista of listless spectres. Abandoned gear and rubbish lie in drifts among the rags of makeshift awnings.

Hasdrubal has survived the battle. The greater part of his troops have survived. After the battle the army moved to higher ground with its baggage and its wounded, to a long arid hilltop. A mile away the deserted battlefield is dense with vultures. They hop and flounce clumsily among the dead. They say that the neck of the vulture is bald, featherless, so that it can crane in and peck out the entrails from the cavity of the carcass more easily.

The Numidian host is encamped around the base of the long hill and the army of Carthage is invested, besieged. Forage parties cannot find a way through the encircling army and besides, the country is empty, a desert.

Masinissa sent a message soon after the battle: a Roman delegation is on its way, arbitrators, peace-keepers. So Hasdrubal waits, forgoes his chance to break out, but no delegation arrives, or if they have arrived and seen that events are running in favour of Numidia, then they have returned home. Dysentery breaks out among the men. The stink of shit is sharp in the throat and the sick are mad for water. Food, water and supplies begin to give out. The old king sends another letter: he will allow the army of Carthage to depart unharmed if they give up the Numidian deserters. Hasdrubal refuses. The dark horsemen, the deserters, sit apart, listless and inert. Few of their horses remain. Mostly they have been eaten. The army has survived on horseflesh and there is bad blood between the mercenaries and the Numidians. For a long time the Africans

66

resisted the killing of their horses, until the Spanish archers began to shoot them from a distance. They lay about twitching and kicking while the black men wept. The morning following, a Spaniard was found with his throat cut. There have been quarrels over the carcasses too, and killings.

The time has passed when the army of Carthage might have broken through the encircling fence of the enemy. The men are sick, starving, and the will to resist has ebbed away through the sultry, windless days. Hasdrubal sends for the Numidian princes, Anasis and Stuba and tells them that he intends to surrender. They make no protest and bow their heads, dead men. It is as if they are somehow redeemed by this retribution, relieved, glad even in some distant part of their unspeaking souls, and make no complaint.

Hasdrubal has sent the spy Qart with a letter asking for the old man's terms and the messenger has returned, picking his way up the stony hillside leading his horse. He makes his way across the hilltop through the squalid encampment of staring ghosts. He offers the sealed package to the fat man as he sits in the ruins of his litter.

'Read it. Read it. Numidian is beyond me.'

The spy breaks open the seal on the bulky package and strips of scarlet chiffon float to the ground. He finds the letter within and reads for a moment in silence.

'Well?'

'The army are to leave the hilltop unarmed and barefoot. They are to walk in a single line, each man wearing only his shirt. He sends red armbands, twenty of them. He guarantees the safety of whoever you choose to wear them.'

'What about the rest? What does he say about my sad thousands, my barrow boys? What does he say about them?'

'Nothing.'

16

Spendios opens his journal by the wooden bookmark and writes rapidly, the characters racing across the page, hatched and jagged.

A catastrophe. Hasdrubal's army has been destroyed. Messengers arrived in the city this morning. As I sit here I can here the sound of lamentation across the rooftops. The sound is everywhere. The library closed early. We were sent home. Everywhere there are crowds befouled with ash. I saw women scratching their faces till the blood ran. I went to see Mara the widow. She was washing clothes in her yard, scrubbing and scrubbing. She did not speak. I am not sure if she saw me at all. Shutters are closed. The city is full of rumour. Hasdrubal is still alive they say and on his way back to the city with a handful of survivors. I heard that the dead number forty thousand, slaughtered by treachery. So many. A catastrophe. The library is closed tomorrow. A day of mourning has been declared. The temples will be full. There will be sacrifices at the Tophet. A catastrophe.

17

Hasdrubal stands pig naked at the tall window of his house in the garden suburb of Megara with the letter in his hands and addresses the shadowed room behind him.

'Yesterday they condemned me to death for losing the war, as they would have condemned me for winning it. And now, today, this. They have given me to understand that I may flee the city at my convenience.'

He gestures with the letter. A fragment of wax from the broken seal skitters across the marble floor. He turns away from the window, haloed by the light, and speaks to the darkness.

'Do not you rebuke me with your silence. I have been through the fire. Do not accuse me.'

'Where are your thousands, husband? Where are the children of the city?'

'What might I have done?'

'You might have died, fought, anything but this.'

'I was betrayed. The city betrayed me, my enemies in the Council of a Hundred betrayed me. You know that.'

'Even a man betrayed can choose.'

'Choose? There are no choices. What you say is false. I despise your falseness. I despise your false, fine-boned aristocratic snobbery. I despise your good form, your cheap patriotism. What can you know? The world out there is a desert where only the carrion birds grow fat. To live is to survive at any cost, is to eat the dead. The living will do anything, anything.'

He has moved across the room to where she stands against the wall in the shadow, has pushed his gross naked body against her. He is a bull, a bear, blind, unformed and shambling in his despair.

'What do you know about survival? What do you know about anything?'

She is pulled about as he tears the clothes from her body. She stumbles to her knees and is pulled up again, trembling violently, her back against the wall. He pushes his fist between her legs and lifts her from the ground on his great forearm, holding her by the throat against the wall with his other hand. Beads from her torn necklace cascade to the marble floor with a sound like rain. He holds her there, up against the wall, a trembling naked doll, crucified, and weeps up at her, roaring like an infant, a beast.

Before the War

18

Cato shuffles the sheets of paper and begins to speak.

'I have recently returned from Carthage, I and my colleagues. I can tell you, gentlemen, that Carthage is a fine city, a fine city, with its wide streets and its public works. Housing for the poor, built at the public expense, puts the stews of Rome to shame. And Carthage is a prosperous city. Its markets and souks overflow with opulent merchandise. All the luxuries of the inhabited world are to be had in the bazaars of Carthage. Jewels, precious metals, spices, slaves, silks. I have seen it. The city of Carthage is a vision of prosperity. There are no beggars on her streets, no limbless veterans of foreign wars.

It is fifty years, gentlemen, fifty years since the great Scipio Africanus placed Rome's boot heel on the neck of the city of Carthage and in the years since then she has exacted the customary revenge of the vanquished. She has grown rich. In the peace we have imposed upon her she has grown rich. We deprived her of the right to maintain an army or a navy. In our wisdom, we deprived her of that expense. Whilst the legions and the navies of Rome have been bleeding our treasury dry, the treasuries of Carthage are filled to overflowing. Such annual reparations as Rome exacted have been paid with ease, with increasing ease. As you are well aware, it is now fifty years since Scipio's victory over the butcher of Carthage, and the last instalment of their tribute has been paid into the public coffers of Rome. Carthage is now free to become still richer, more opulent, more insolent in her wealth.

The question we must ask ourselves, gentlemen, is this. Is the city of Carthage the friend or the enemy of the city of Rome? That is the question we must address. If we listen to the Carthaginian ambassadors we can be in no doubt. Carthage intends us no harm. She has paid her tribute. Indeed, she has offered to supply our armies abroad with shiploads of corn, free of charge. She is a trading city, like any other, a city of honest, honourable merchants. Live and let live, say the Carthaginians. Carthage is not the enemy of Rome, say the Carthaginians.

Indeed, there are those in this house who will aver that it matters not a jot whether Carthage is our enemy or not. An enemy on the doorstep, in the opinion of these sages, is in very truth a good thing. With an enemy at the gate, they say, we are not so inclined to squabble amongst ourselves. I must confess, gentlemen, that this elevated wisdom is altogether too subtle for my simple soldier's brains

Let me say a word to you, gentlemen. One word.

That word is Trasimene.

At the battle of Trasimene, in which so many of your grand-fathers, your fathers and uncles sacrificed themselves for the father-land, eighty thousand Romans died at the hands of Carthaginian troops. The flower of our manhood went into the pit on that day. But Carthage is not the enemy of Rome.

Let me say a word to you, another word.

That word is Cannae.

On a single day the army of Hannibal slaughtered a generation. My father died at Cannae, on that fatal riverbank.

Who can forget the spectre of one-eyed Hannibal and his cut throats? The South of Italy is still a desert of empty villages and towns. For twelve years the butcher of Carthage ravaged our country, turned it into a wasteland.

But Carthage is not the enemy of Rome. They are merchants in Carthage, peace-loving men. Live and let live, say the Carthaginians. We have given over our warlike ways, they say, learnt wisdom, humility. We are content to be Rome's vassal, eager to do her bidding.

Gentlemen, they are lying.

I have seen the proof of it with my own eyes.

Item: Carthage has built a wall around its harbours, or should I say, a fortress.

Item: Carthage has a shipyard within this fortress that could build a fleet in a year, a war fleet.

Item: Carthage is even now laying plans to wage covert war against our ally Masinissa, using paid mercenaries and levies of its own citizens, against the express interdict of this Senate.

Gentlemen, let me show you something. Indulge me. Let me show you some figs. I bought these figs in the market this morning and they are excellent figs. These are succulent figs. These figs were picked three days ago, in Carthage. In Carthage, gentlemen. We have an enemy three days from our gates.

Gentlemen, I say to you now, and from today I shall say it each and every time I enter this chamber. I believe that Carthage must be destroyed. I believe that Carthage must be destroyed.'

The old man puts down his speech and pinches the bridge of his nose. Reading makes his eyes water these days. He looks across to where the slaves are pruning the fruit trees in the sunshine.

'What do you think?'

Harpax is sitting beside him on the bench, picking at a thread. He is wearing a labourer's hat, against the heat of the sun.

'It is an excellent speech. You are to be congratulated.'

'But will it do the job? Will it convince them?'

'Some are convinced already. I think that the Senate is coming round to your view. A solution must be found to the Carthaginian question, a final solution. Tell me about the figs.'

'The figs? Nice touch, don't you think?'

'Is it true? Can you really buy figs in Rome that were picked three days ago in Carthage?'

'Damned if I know. This is rhetoric. I shall pick them here in the garden, and take them in to the Senate with me tomorrow.'

19

The Campus Martius, the Field of Mars, is enclosed to the west by a bend of the Tiber. The river loops invisibly beyond expanses of rough grass. Only the masts of the lighters passing upriver from Ostia to the wharves of the city give a clue to its presence. To the South and East the city is a scrawl of tenements beneath the ramparts of the Capitol. Along the eastern edge of the Field of Mars runs the Via Flaminia, paved with grey pumice. A funeral cortège moves imperceptibly along the road as it leaves the city for the graveyards of Pincius. Plumed black horses draw the bier. Mourners walk behind, and behind them, hired actors wearing the death masks of the ancestors, pace magisterially. A picture painted on a vase.

Time out of mind the Field of Mars is where the armies of Rome have gathered. In the old days it was farmers from the villages and towns of Latium, citizen soldiers coming to defend the native land, forming up in their centuries in the long grass where springtime breezes ran. Winter for ploughing: Summer for campaigning. And then came the long years of Hannibal's terror, when the dead outnumbered the living and all the young men went down into the pit, and the army of Rome was reduced to an army of old men, slaves, foreigners and criminals. These days, soldiers fight for money, for the chance of gain.

Recruiting for the Carthage campaign is brisk. Carthage is an opulent city, everyone knows that, a city of fat defenceless moneylenders. The sack of Carthage is a vision that entices. Today is the day when the new levies will form up in their centuries and take the oath. Peasants, small farmers fleeing the poverty of the land, abandoning their smallholdings, have accepted the Senate's shilling. There is no living to be made on the land when half the country is given over to slave-run estates. Prices have been ruined. On his own farm a free man can no longer eat. Today these poor men will become soldiers. They will be led by the rich. It is the universal economy of war. The poor are led to suffering and death by the rich. How could it be different?

They will be marched away to their camps for basic training. They will be issued with heavy boots, a heavy sword and shield, javelins, entrenching tools, armour, helmet, and they will pay for them in arrears out of their wages. Soldiers are, first of all, beasts of burden. On the march a legionary will carry more than half of his own weight in equipment and food. Mules: that is the word the legionaries use about themselves.

In the weeks that follow, the new levies will be marched forward and back on dusty parade grounds by dour centurions and shrill corporals. They will learn to march in step, to wheel, turn, about face, to run in step. They will learn a particular obedience, a precise, unthinking obedience. In their cohorts and centuries they will learn how to transform the column of march to a line, to a square, to a phalanx. They will learn the economy of the sword, the rule of the short blow, the chop, the thrust. In, twist, out. One, two, three. They will learn to do these things in step, in implacable, scissoring ranks. They will learn a particular obedience, an obedience edged and hedged about by retribution and death. The penalty for sleeping on duty is death. The penalty for cowardice is death. The penalty for unauthorised looting is death. The penalty for wilful disobedience is death. The penalty for insubordination is a hundred strokes of the cane. A soldier absent from roll call must eat his meals standing up for a month.

It is early morning. The centurions, the career men, their grizzled heads shaved like nuts, are directing the setting out of flags, marking out the broad empty fields with pennants, coloured and numbered, so that the gathering of the new legions will be an orderly thing, a precise thing, and every man will have his place. By the end of the day, the infantry of six new legions will have gathered here, taken the oath and departed, twenty four thousand souls. They will straggle to this place in their hesitant groups, gripping their poor bundles, simple men, peasants, bankrupt farmers, driven from their little patches of scratched earth under the onslaught of the time. They will leave this place in impassive ranks, eyes to the front: legionaries, mules. The cavalry, the artillery will come later. Other legions, the fourth, the tenth, the sixth Dalmatiae, hardened men, are on their way back from Spain and Greece.

The centurions move about distantly in the grey drizzle of morning. A group of junior staff officers sit their horses, young men nursing hangovers, while the thin rain beads the pile of their expensive cloaks.

'I say.'

Antoninus Pius is twenty-two and has made a good start on squandering his inheritance. He was, briefly, on active service in Spain, but the heat didn't suit him so he wrote to his mother, who used her connections, and now he is back in Rome. He spends his time at the bath-house gambling, at the theatre and the brothel. In the mornings he takes a turn or two around the Forum to keep abreast of the gossip. He has volunteered for the Carthage campaign. He has bought a commission at an inflated price but the investment is secure. The Carthage business will be over in a season and the pickings will be phenomenal if half the talk in the Forum is to be believed. He has a troubling dose of the pox which makes sitting his horse in the rain a bit of a trial.

'I say.'

He catches a corporal's eye. The man runs up, salutes.

'Sir.'

'What exactly are those items?'

He points to a distant part of the fields where sheep are grazing.

'Er... sheep... sir.'

'Sheep?'

The note of incredulity is nicely calculated. It is instantly understood that the presence of the sheep is the corporal's fault.

'Sir.'

'Well, soldier, I want you to get rid of those sheep. This is the Campus fucking Martius, the Field of Mars. We've got a delegation of Yids coming out here, Carthaginian top brass, and I'm supposed to impress them with the military might of Rome, and there are sheep all over the fucking place. What is this, toytown? Get rid of them, do you hear? Get rid of them.'

'Sir.'

The corporal runs off, brow furrowed. A few moments later a squad of privates, who have been given to understand that the presence of sheep on the Field of Mars is entirely their responsibility, are moving across the grass in skirmishing order, their brows furrowed.

Antoninus Pius will die on the walls of Carthage, tied to a post, disembowelled in full view of his men. The last thing he will see are his own insides coiling at his feet.

Afternoon. The Field of Mars is no longer empty. It is a wide sea of humanity, a milling vista. Lines of men stretch as far as the eye can see. The margin between order and chaos seems indistinct. The confusion is illusory. In every direction the centuries are beginning to cohere, to take on the form of an army. All day the new recruits have been coming in from their villages and towns, from nights spent in cheap hostels in the city, from nights spent in hayricks and ditches. The straggling crowds become straggling lines. The lines grow in length, they swell, grow straight: ranks of four, twenty men deep, centuries. The organism begins to evolve toward the machine. Centurions and NCOs are pushing and shouting, comparing lists. New arrivals are drifting in all the time. Young officers, hardly more than boys, canter their thoroughbred horses down the flagged avenues of trampled grass with their despatches, sitting very straight in the saddle and careful to keep their eyes to the front. Somewhere a military band is playing. The sound drifts like music at a summer showground. Away by the Via Flaminia, the general staff are sitting on canvas chairs on a temporary podium, surveying the gathering of the locust storm.

Marcus Manilius is well pleased with himself as he sits on his upholstered chair with his Consul's baton across his knees. To have been elected Consul for this campaign is good fortune indeed. Not cheap good fortune, but good fortune nonetheless. Nothing comes of nothing. Already the list of gifts and donations from aspiring officers is long and will get longer if he keeps on deferring the appointment of staff officers. His own not inconsiderable debts are nearly paid. They say that it is all but impossible to persuade ambitious young officers to take up appointments with the armies in Spain when this war is about to be fought. Of course, nothing has been said, nothing is official. There is no word of it from the Senate. Nervous Carthaginian ambassadors are perplexed by the noncommittal tone which has crept into diplomatic relations. They meet their opposite numbers at functions on the Capitol in the usual way and somehow nothing is said. Conversation slides away from the substantive, the particular. The Carthaginian diplomats stationed in Rome keep a close ear on foreign news and would like to be comforted by what they hear. Roman armies have overrun Macedon, and Perseus the king is no longer a player, but the cities of Macedon have been spared. Macedon is taxed cruelly, it is true, but her cities have been spared. The armies of Rome are crowding south into Greece. Epirus has been enslaved. The cities of the Achaean league are defecting to Rome every day. And these cities are being spared. Surely Carthage will be spared. The rumours cannot be true. What would it profit the city of Rome to rekindle a war after fifty years of peace? Surely Carthage will be spared.

In the Forum gossip feeds on official silence, runs wild along forking paths. Rome will ally with the Numidians against Carthage. Carthage will ally with Numidia against Rome. Rome will ally with Carthage against Numidia. Masinissa the Numidian king, who is a hundred and ten, has fathered triplets. One of them has two heads, as god is my judge.

In the barracks and in the officers' mess the word is out that this war will make everyone rich. Everyone knows that Carthage will crack like an egg and her riches will spill out upon her conquerors. They will all become heroes overnight. Children will sleep at night because the evil empire will have been overthrown. The spectre of Hannibal will have been exorcised at last. To be there at the kill is the stuff of dreams. Marcus Manilius is exploiting these dreams, feeding these fires of ambition by the simple device of deferring appointments. The bidding grows brisker by the day. He fingers the filigree of his Consular baton and smiles as the mules assemble out there in their thousands on the Field of Mars.

20

'This,' says the gigantic bosun, holding a heavy leather loop above his shaved-to-the-bone head, 'is ay twister. What is it sailor?'

He raises his eyebrows archly at a wretch on the front row.

'A twister.'

'Ay twister. And what sort of ay twister, sailor, would you say it was?'

The wretch gives off a sullen, frightened silence.

'This, sailor is ay twister, *sir*. Take this item away and give him ten with the rope's end.'

The bosun's brutes drag the man away, his manacles clattering on the decking. The bosun hangs the leather strap from his finger end.

'What sort of ay twister, sailor?

His eye is on the man to the right of the gap on the front row.

'A twister... sir.'

'Very quick. We'll make a sailor of you yet. And it is called ay twister for the simple reason that we twist it. Like so.'

He turns the strap into a figure of eight above his head.

'And one bight of *thee* twister, one loop as a landsman would say, goes over thee thole pin.'

The bosun steps across the deck to a rower's bench. He drops the twisted strap neatly over the curved wooden peg which is set into the bulwark.

'What does it go over, sailor?'

His eye returns to the same man.

' The thole pin...'

The playwright is sitting next to him, his eyes forward, expressionless. His elbow makes a small sudden movement sideways.

'...sir.'

The bosun's fearsome brow registers slight unconscious unease for an instant.

'Quite right, sailor. The thole pin, sir. And the other bight, the other loop, goes over the oar itself.'

The huge man hefts a fourteen foot oar from the deck and slips it through the strap with practised, ostentatious ease. He slips it down to the painted marker and abandons it with theatrical carelessness, letting it hang over the side and into the water of the dock.

'By this simple means *thee* oar is secured to thee vessel. Also it prevents wear on *thee* valuable timbers of thee gunwale. The ships of the Roman Navy are of great value, whereas you...'

The bosun scans his half starved and stinking audience.

'...are of no value at all. What are you of, sailor?'

His deliberate glance falls on the playwright.

'No value at all...... sir.'

The pause is calculated to an almost fatal nicety. The brows furrow dangerously but the bosun cannot quite place his perplexity.

'In fact you are thee dregs. What are you, sailor?'

'*Thee* dregs......sir.'

The bosun's meat cleaver face blurs for a long moment in unlocatable unease. He clears his throat, clearing the faintly troubled deck of his mind, and continues.

'Such is the generosity of *thee* Roman Naval Authorities that each man will be issued with ay twister free of charge. This valuable item will be numbered and marked down to each oarsman by name. The first man to lose his twister over the side will be flogged for an entire watch and then dropped over the side to join *thee* lost item. Do I make myself clear?

Thee second item which will be issued to each man, entirely free of charge, at the public expense, is this.'

He holds up above his head a padded square of leather with straps attached to its corners.

'This is *thee* oarsman's mat or cushion, which goes beneath the rower's arse, thus preventing splinters, chafing, soreness, boils, piles and other ailments to which oarsmen are susceptible. *Thee* Roman Naval Authorities do not give a toss if you drop your mat over the side. The welfare of your arse is entirely your concern. But believe me, my jolly sailor boys, you will row whether your arse bleeds or not. You will row if it drops off. You will come to love your rower's mat more than your own mother.'

The quinquereme *Bellerophon* displaces seventy-five tons. She is sixteen feet in the beam and one hundred and twenty feet long, a sleek arrow of a vessel. A short mast amidships carries a lateen sail for use in the open sea. In battle she is driven by three hundred oarsmen. The long bladed pinewood oars are more than twice the height of a man. At her bow the bronze-clad beak basks like a shark just below the surface. The impact at ramming speed of warships in this class is considerable and an enemy vessel will founder within minutes after a successful attack. Ten years ago the Roman warship *Bellerophon* was the Greek warship *Aletheia*, drifting with only her sternpost and broken mast showing above the surface of the Athenian Sea and the swollen corpses of forty oarsmen bobbing against the timbers beneath the deck. The *Aletheia* had foundered instantly, rammed below the waterline amidships in a minor and unrecorded engagement with a Delian squadron. The foundered ship drifted for a week before being towed to Piraeus for repair. With the fall of the Achaean League to the armies of Rome she was beached, under the terms of the surrender. Three months ago she was rowed to Italy by an Egyptian delivery crew on the written order of a civil servant in Rome, with no explanation given. She is one of fifty warships and a hundred transports commandeered during the past months from Greek and Macedonian ship owners without explanation, or payment.

The *Bellerophon* has three tiers of rowers' benches along each side. The lowest tier is below the level of the deck and the oar ports are only two feet above the surface of the water when the ship is carrying her full complement of men. The oar ports on the lower tier are each fitted with a leather apron which is secured by a drawstring to the oar. These aprons keep out the worst of the seas when they are in good repair though the oarsmen on the windward side generally row naked to keep the chafing salt out of what clothes they possess. The oars used by the men on the lower tier are shorter and the thalamioi as they are known, the bilge rowers, manage an oar apiece.

The oars of the upper two tiers are longer and are worked by two men apiece. When rowing, the heads of the bilge men are at a level with the decking and a little below the backsides of the oarsmen on the middle tier. Bilge men are students of the farts of the middle tier men, the zygioi, and traditionally there is little love lost between them. The benches of the upper tier are set outboard above the water on a wooden outrigger and the sea passes a yard beneath the oarsmen's feet. The upper tier men, the thranitai, are the obscure aristocrats of this fearsome trade. The management of the outermost oar requires particular strength and skill. The thranitai are the stroke men and their deep outbreath chant as they pull is the ship's heartbeat. The oarsmen on the lower tiers give their voices to the return stroke. It is the anthem of the ship, the song of the long labour of the blood.

The playwright stands in line naked to have his head shaved. He is issued with a leather twister and a bench mat. His name and age are entered in a ledger by a clerk with a hare lip who spells badly. It turns out that since he is not a slave but a reprieved criminal he is entitled to wages, not much, a few denarii each month, but something. He is not merely a chattel of the Republic but a man with a profession and this thought restores to him the unexpected outlines of an identity. He is not quite sure in his mind that the hare lipped clerk hasn't made a mistake.

Since he was reborn into the bloody sunlight of the arena, since he felt the key turn in the lock of his muffled and private purgatory and suffered the burst of white roaring light, he has been a mirror, a sentient absence, a passing shadow of sensation cast upon the time, existing without expectation or regret. But now he is somebody, an oarsman, a professional, at right angles to the world. His luck sees him again.

The new conscripts are ferried out in lighters on a grey blustery afternoon to the *Bellerophon* as she rides at anchor a mile from the shore. Half the complement of oarsmen is already aboard, experienced men, corded with sinew, and each new man is allocated to an experienced man. The playwright finds himself on the upper tier, with the sea banging and slapping a yard below his feet, sitting next to a naked black African whose every inch of muscle-roped flesh is pierced and scarified. Unexpectedly, soaking spray cannons upward. The playwright takes off his clothes. Without comment his companion takes the half sodden bundle and stows it in an oiled canvas bag below the bench. The playwright sits at his bench gazing at the foreshortened row of backs curving away toward the high sternpost. He sees the stroke man take his place at the drum. The bosun materialises like an evil genie. He paces the deck, end to end, at his leisure, taking stock of his three hundred, gathers himself, clears his throat and spits, tests the rope's end against the forward rail......

Each blue dawn they go out, the three hundred, in lighters whose holds are still ankle deep in Egyptian corn, commandeered from the port of Ostia, and take their places on the benches of the *Bellerophon*. In the half light they file aboard the vessel in two long lines, advancing down the deck and dropping into the confines of their customary benches. Space is tight. They row until it is dark, quartering the wide sea, until the playwright hangs over the oar in blank, stunned exhaustion. His partner, his African, pours water on his head without comment.

The playwright's hands blister, bleed, half heal, break open again. His hands are little worlds of pain in the larger agony of his body. His companion binds the bleeding palms with strips of canvas. The bindings grow stiff, blood brown and the scarlet seeps.

He learns to pull by the hour, learns to respond to the stroke drum as if it were his own heart, the voice of his own body, learns to exist in the collective roar of the pull and the roar of the return, learns to back water, to ship the long oar with a thoughtless heft. He learns to pause with the oar blade dripping, and to pull again, machinelike and on the instant, at the sound of the boatswain's stentorian O opop! O opop! O opop! He finds it in himself to sustain the pace of the ram through chest-bursting transcendental minutes while the stroke drum commands inhuman, impossible, pitiless momentum and the sea beneath his feet is churning furrowed spume: the rum dum, the rum dum, the rum dum, the rum dum, the rum dum.....

As the long days pass into weeks he begins to glimpse obscure redemption, the simple unsayable salvation that comes with work. He learns the dark exultation of effort and is somewhere redeemed. Rowing through the hours his body finds a way to its own economy, to its fitness for purpose. They row together, he and his black other, his philosopher, his familiar. The playwright rows until the heavy oar is hardly more than an extension of thought, and he a stylite, a hermit of the oar itself. He becomes the bone's engine, the creature of his own sinew. He rows, eats, shits like an automaton and sleeps dreamless in sudden black oblivion.

Not all of the new men survive to hear the voice of the oar. In the first days the sick and the weak go under, collapse and are tipped over the side. Sometimes they break in their minds and fall into staring catalepsy so that their hands must be prized from the oar. They go over the side unspeaking. The playwright watches below his feet an upturned uncomprehending face moving toward the stern in the oars' urgent swell.

In the rowers' harsh caste system the playwright maintains his place of privilege on the upper tier among the professionals, the paid men. His African has underwritten his presence there, led him to his hard salvation. With his first wages he buys barley bread, a water skin, a net of onions from the bumboat.

Below him on the lower tiers the bosun and his mates prowl and curse but on the upper tier, out over the flying water they row in some untouchable, defiant space. They spend themselves because it is in them to do it, because it is their pleasure, because to do less would be the way of the pauper.

The *Bellerophon* is not the only ship on that sea. Other crews are being put through it. The playwright, who once knew nothing of these things, distinguishes them at a glance: quinqueremes, triremes, fifty oared penteconters. He can tell a vessel built in Piraeus from a Delian ship. He has become a student of the game, with a critic's eye for technique, morale, power.

A hundred yards on the starboard side of the *Bellerophon* a trireme pulls level, a long black ship with a baleful eye painted on the prow, the *Meltemi: Piraeus*. The crew are Greeks, professionals, oarsmen of the disbanded Achaean fleet, mercenaries now. In the barracks they set themselves apart with their surly diffidence. National humiliation cuts deep and they take badly to the jeering of the Italians. Out here on the sea this is their game, flaunting their easy skills, rowing with insolent precision, goading the scratch crews, keeping exactly abreast and mouthing obscenities across the scintillating water, showing their arses. The bow officer is lounging with thespian carelessness above the painted eye against the tall cutwater. The long three-tiered mill of oars rises and falls in a calculated display of sneering, well practised machismo. One of the *Bellerophon's* bilge rowers pushes a gargoyle face through his oar port.

'Fuck off, arse bandits. We don't want none.'

The playwright is watching the bosun as the big man measures his chances. The bosun is between a rock and a hard place. The Greeks have been playing this game with the new scratch crews for days, taunting them to race and then pulling effortlessly ahead the moment the challenge is taken up. Too fast to race against they are altogether too arrogant and shit-faced to ignore. Minutes pass and the two rams nose level under the blue water. The pace is unhurried. The oar banks rise and fall in unison. The bosun cannot decide. His predicament is acute. Like Burridan's ass, the playwright thinks, likely to perish of indecision. The taunt hangs like a gull in the space between the ships.

The playwright catches his African's eye for the flicker of a moment. Complicity is instantaneous. With one voice they call out the new stroke. O opop! O opop! O opop! O opop! The oars dip automatically in response and the *Bellerophon*, as it seems, of its own volition, begins slowly to draw ahead. The crew have been hanging over the instant and they give way with a will. A hundred yards off the *Meltemi* is a machine, oars rising and falling in fearful symmetry. She draws inexorably and effortlessly level again. The bosun has no choices left. He picks up the beater and takes up the quickening measure on the drum. The ships drive outward, arrowing out of twin white wakes.

The land has dropped away and the red clouds of evening are gathering along the horizon. The men of the *Bellerophon* are rowing. The oarsmen on the starboard side hardly glance across now to the doppelganger, to the mirrored rise and fall of the *Meltemi's* oars. It is hours into the game and the rules are drifting. The men of the *Bellerophon* are rowing now because they are rowing. The bosun knows they will not give over. The beater hangs in his hand. His three hundred are rowing in the deep and causeless place. They are chanting the stroke. It is the anthem of the ship, the song of the long labour of the blood. Tears are running down his face.

Ten hours out. The bosun squints into the black night. The Greek is still there, her bows still level. In the distant darkness a line of faint phosphorescence glimmers where the oars dip. His oarsmen are rowing in half hour watches now: an hour on, half an hour off. He does not think of anything, does not even wonder when the Greek will turn back.

In the paling dawn the *Bellerophon* is crossing an empty sea. A wandering fulmar slips in and out of the swells ahead of the breaking bow wave. The horizon is empty. The *Meltemi* is nowhere, fallen back, lost over the horizon.

21

This morning I walked through the agora on my way to the library. The place was packed, buzzing like a wasps' nest. The town of Utica up the coast from here has sent an embassy to Rome. It seems the Utican city council have offered what they call 'deditio' which means that the Romans can do as they like with the place. Utica has given itself to Rome. People were saying that the Uticans could see which way the wind was blowing. In the last war their loyalty to Carthage cost them dear. There are old people there who still remember the war. With the Romans on one side and the Numidians on the other Carthage is between the hammer and the anvil. They were saying that the luck of Carthage has run out.

It seems odd somehow. You can walk there in a day to Utica. I know a man who goes there on a Sunday to go fishing. People here in the city have family connections there, cousins, nieces and nephews. Mother has a cousin there. Utica is a Phoenician town, like Carthage. The people are the same. They worship the same gods, sing the same songs. Utica still sends gift ships to the temples in Tyre the same as we do.

On my way home from the library I stopped off for a few minutes to see Mara the widow. Her son didn't come back last year from the war against the Numidians. One of the many. Sometimes it seems as if there are no young men left in the city. Her hands are red from her work in the laundry. She wipes them on her apron all the time. Big hands she has, bony and raw looking. Her eyes are round and white, red rimmed. She has the eyes of a horse. Her house is scrubbed and empty. She lost her husband years ago and now the boy is dead too, her only one. I didn't stay long.

Spendios closes his journal and sits a moment with his eyes closed, the bridge of his nose pinched between finger and thumb, then turns again to what he should be doing. It is a fat codex, its folded pages falling like a concertina across the table: the Annual

Report of the Clerk to the Roman Tribunate. Dull stuff. He translates a lot of the official documents which come down the routine diplomatic channels for the attention of the Council of One Hundred. His translations go to an assortment of standing committees who have offices in Carthage's parliament buildings. Only he reads them all. His knowledge of the Roman official mind is deep. In Carthage he has a unique grasp of the labyrinth of Roman officialdom and of the dark recesses of its collective mind. He is of course never consulted. He was born into the wrong caste. The Baals, the old families, rarely look beyond their own ranks. Preferment is jealously guarded, hedged about by the proscriptions of traditional caste law and the instincts of the self. The soothing sound of rioting apprentices comes up from the lower town through hot summer nights to the sumptuous town houses on the Byrsa. The families sit on their terraces under their silk awnings high over the mean streets watching the moon rise over the burnished sea, and the roar of distant riot in the lower town is oddly reassuring to them.

In the years he has been translating these official Roman documents Spendios has become aware of a drift in the Latin itself, a movement away from the tersely practical, the matter-of-fact, toward some other idiom heavy with authority. In little epiphanies of shifted usage he has begun to sense something self-aware, obscurely peremptory, inhuman even. As he works his way year by year through the blockish texts, the dull resolutions and edicts, the rulings and official recommendations, foreboding weeps ever more freely from the flicker of the script. Foreign policy has grown inflexible. There is no pity in them. It is as if they wished to rule the world for a thousand years. References to the city of Carthage are few enough: mercantile rulings mostly, a tightening of customs regulations, a raising of import duties. When they occur, these references, he is aware of a faint sensation in his stomach.

Sometimes he has to stop working, to pause, to close the document and let his mind rest, let clenched apprehension ebb a little, let the darkness lift.

22

The paved road that leads from Rome to Ostia and the coastal ports is solid with carts and columns of men. These are the new men, the mules, trudging beneath the weight of their packs. Prices are high in the port of Ostia. There is not a room to be had. The waterfront is alive with activity day and night. Chandlers' boats and lighters cluster round the transport galleys, while the warships, the invasion fleet, rides at anchor a mile out beyond the river mouth. The *Bellerophon* has been ordered in to the port itself. The oarsmen manoeuvre the long vessel through the crowded shipping on the river. She is made fast to the wharf at the berth which has been cleared for her.

When the oarsmen return from their new barracks to the ship the following morning they are ordered to stand to on the quayside. Striped awnings and a sort of pavilion have been installed on the deck. There are chairs and tables fastened to the decking. There is a coming and going of slaves with silverware, boxes and baskets. The oarsmen speculate.

'Obvious. Every invasion fleet needs one, and the *Bellerophon*, the very jewel in the fleet's crown has been chosen.'

'What are you on about?'

'Well, stands to reason. It's the only crew with the necessary moral calibre for the job.'

'What is this man on about?'

'Look. Use your eyes. What does all this say to you, the stripy awnings, the silverware, the bedding?

'Go on then. What does it say?'

'It says 'brothel', that's what it says. We are going to be rowing the expedition brothel. A floating house of pleasure.'

'You are out of your tree.'

'You wait. You just wait. They'll be here anytime. Hundreds of 'em there'll be. Tall ones with huge tits and long blonde hair.

'...short ones with big bums and false eyelashes...'

'...and jewels in their belly buttons...'

'...big puckery nipples...'

They wait. The hours pass. Their heated visions do not materialise. They are given the order to fall out. They sit under the long shadow of one of the warehouses which line the river front. The knucklebones come out, the dice. Some sleep in the noon shade, unheard of luxury, and all the while men and materials are passing out to the ships in the bay. Slaves bounce along gangplanks to the lighters under improbably large sacks. Mules, new men just out of basic training, stand under their loads in the white sunlight waiting for the barges in impassive columns of four, century by century along the wharf as far as the eye can see. When it is their turn to go they clamber down the netting into the barge and reform in columns of four. Eyes to the front. No talking that man. The barges come and go through the morning and the afternoon and still the lines of infantrymen stretch out of sight. When it grows dark, the oarsmen are marched back to the barracks past the waiting columns.

The next morning things are different. There are guards posted along the wharf by the *Bellerophon* and a clutch of immaculate house slaves on the deck. In the cool by the warehouse the oarsmen wait again. About noon there is a stir and army staff officers begin to appear down the quay, gorgeous young men in their bespoke uniforms. The infantry waiting to embark stiffen as they pass. The young officers pause by the gangplank in self-conscious tableaux. Individuals crane back along the quay. In the shade the oarsmen are all eyes. They nudge one another.

'See, I told you. A military escort. Must be high class whores..'

'Bollocks.'

'Sweet Janus!'

'What? What?'

'Look.'

'What?'

'It's the General bleeding Staff, the top brass.'

'Where? Where?'

'Look, that's whatshisname. You know, the Consul... Censorinus.'

'And that must be the other bugger, the tall weedy one.

The splendid entourage arrives by the gangplank of the *Bellerophon*. There is a pausing, a moment of nervousness among these young patricians. Beneath the gravitas a hint of theatricality. The officers who have already arrived are introduced to the two

Consuls. There is saluting and a formal nodding of plumed helmets, a certain calculated flourishing of Consular batons. Censorinus has the fleet, Manilius the army, career politicians both of them. Manilius served as a tribune in Spain and came back under a cloud, they say. Censorinus is a rich boy, a nobody with a weak chin. But they each carry the Consular baton. The dignity, as they say, is in the office, not the man. Their families, their wives and children, wait under parasols held by slaves for the formal leave-taking.

Scipio Aemilianus arrives late. He comes down the dockside with Cornelia his adopted grandmother on his arm and his younger sister Clodia walking behind. Cornelia has the straight back of old money. There are slaves carrying baskets and boxes. Aemilianus chats to the old woman as they walk as if it were a picnic party. They pause by the ship while the slaves go aboard with the luggage.

Clodia is staring about. She has a thin boyish look and her grandmother's erect carriage. She sees him immediately, the last man standing. It is her dream. He is standing in the long line of his fellows in the shadows. There is no doubt. His head begins to turn. It is her dream. He sees her. She is in the white light of his gaze. Without having moved she is standing in front of him. Later she will remember the wind-burned face, the corded muscle in his neck, the uncertainty in his expression; as if he were trying to bring something to mind. She says, because something must be said, even in the white light.

'I saw your play.'

He cannot place the words, cannot place himself in relation to them. His voice when he speaks, is burred, throaty from lack of use.

'My play?'

Still he cannot place the words, cannot find a context for them. She tries to help him.

'*The General*. It was very funny. We all laughed.'

She can hear her own voice out of the white light as if it were another's.

'And then I saw you in the arena. You were covered in blood.'

Her eyes are swimming. Dark feeling wells up like illness or death. His gaze is a dark place now, a tunnel. There is no time. She senses the approach of feet across the quay. Her mouth is trying to make the shape of a word, but there are no words for what she needs to say.

91

He is trying to understand but there is no time to make him understand. Her brother's slaves are at her elbow, insistent. She is standing in an insupportable breach of public decorum, in an open gateway through which the gale of scandal is blowing.

They take her by the arms as if she were of unsound mind. She is Eurydice, borne away.

23

Today they came for the hostages. The Romans had ordered that only children of the Baals, the families, were acceptable. Three hundred hostages, to be taken to Sicily and then to Rome. Nobody knows what will happen to them. Nobody has been told.

They came down to the harbour, the ones who had been chosen, with their nurses and their families, bundled up in furs and carrying their travel bags. It was a cold day. The oldest of them can't have been more than twelve. The sea front was closed to the public but no one had thought of the sea wall behind. You could still get along the top of the wall. There were hundreds of us on the rampart above them like a crowd at a play. There were two Roman ships moored to the sea wall and soldiers drawn up next to the ships. Things seemed to take a very long time. Everyone seemed to be waiting. Families were standing about in groups. The dockside was filling up as more of them arrived. In the end the Roman officers began to shout and some of the soldiers made a line. They pushed the families back to make a space on the harbour side by the ships. They kept pushing and the families at the back who couldn't see what was happening wouldn't move and the crowd was packed tight. Some of the children were crying and a fight broke out between two men near the back of the crowd. There were Roman officers with lists and the children were checked off and led into the space that had been cleared behind the spears. They had to duck under the spears with their luggage.

A girl stumbled and her bag came open and spilled out. A hairbrush came out and she missed it as she gathered her things together. I watched it, the hairbrush. My eyes kept returning to it, forgotten like that on the flagstones. It seemed very ordinary really, at first, just something that happened. The children stood in the cleared space near the ships with their luggage and the families were crowded against the spears as if it were they who were being imprisoned. It seemed to happen very slowly. I saw a woman straightening her son's hair, smoothing it down before the boy passed under the spears. She never kissed him. The children came through in ones and twos: a brother and a sister holding hands: two sisters, twins, carrying a bag between them. A little boy came through on his own and began to cry. Behind the spears there was a kind of surging.

They kept coming through. There seemed to be so many of them and all so quiet and well behaved. They stood up, all of them, all of the children. None of them sat down on their luggage. I don't think I saw any of them even speak. It was as if they felt that something was expected of them, that somehow they needed to be on their best behaviour, as if it were a Sunday. There was more waiting. Half a dozen soldiers came down about half way along, herding the crowd of children into two parts. It looked for a moment as if the two twins would be separated. And then they began to herd them up the gangways with their bags and cases on to the two ships. I saw a child carrying a case which had his name painted on it. Sholto. How ordinary, somehow, it all was. There was no centre, no focus, no moment to seize upon that was beyond bearing.

And then a child began to cry. It was a boy. He was half way along the gangway, one of the last. Maybe he had looked down, seen the darkness of the water below him. Who knows. It was a thin tearing sound, like the tearing of a veil. Things came to pieces suddenly. The line of soldiers simply dissolved, burst, and the nurses and the mothers came through into the empty space. The soldiers by the gangplanks had drawn their swords. There was nothing the women could do but wail and tear at themselves. I saw women falling in front of the soldiers, begging and weeping and clinging to their legs with their outstretched fingers. Some just stood looking at the ships and tearing at themselves with their nails until they bled. The spear soldiers were pushing past them, scrambling to get back to the ships. Dockworkers were trying to cast off the moorings and the women were dragging at them, holding on to the ropes. Sailors on board were pushing the ships clear of the harbour wall with long poles. A gangplank fell into the water. A woman was clinging to the ship as it moved away. She fell into the narrow space between the ship and the dockside. I saw another woman...

The scribe pauses with his pen poised over the hastily scribbled words. He watches his hand shaking.

24

For a brief period, a few weeks, the *Bellerophon* becomes the expedition flagship. The Consular pennant flutters at the masthead and there is a coming and going of staff officers along the quayside. The ship remains at her berth and the oarsmen are put to work as stevedores on the dock loading grain sacks on to the big transports. On the deck of the *Bellerophon* earnest staff officers pore over maps spread out and weighted down on the fixed tables. Guards are posted on the dockside by the gangplank. Censorinus spends his days under his awning discreetly negotiating bribes in exchange for the vacant commissions that remain.

After a week humping sacks the oarsmen are marched down again in the early dawn to the ship. The dock is silent, fogged and chill, the surface of the water a dim smoking mirror. Voices sound strangely in the mist. The ship is poled away from the berth, moving like a funeral barge in the vague twilight, and the long banks of oars slide out in unison and clash through the mirror. They edge the ship between brooding hulks and out into the river. In the first russet light of daybreak they are pulling for the open sea and the sound of their chanting goes out across the wide waters. As the *Bellerophon* comes slowly away from the coast the ships of the invasion fleet weigh their anchors one by one, too many to count.

The fleet makes the crossing to Sicily under sail in a brisk breeze. The coast, a grey green smudge on the port side, recedes to nothing. The playwright watches tribune Aemilianus who is berthed on the *Bellerophon* hang nervously from the ratlines attempting unhandily to shit into the sea. The playwright knows his name, knows that it was the tribune's sister who spoke to him on the dockside. The incident hangs in his mind like the memory of a dream, troubling and unresolved.

For the oarsmen things improve. Rations are suddenly better: salt meat and figs in addition to the staple black bread and olives. The crossing to Sicily is made in a leisurely three days and the *Bellerophon* drops anchor in the roadstead of Lilybaeum.

When the Consul has gone ashore with his retinue, the crew are taken to the civic baths in Lilybaeum town. As the bemused bosun points out: 'His holiness thee Consul can't abide thee reek no more.' The playwright and his African sit at the edge of the pool in the echoing tepidarium of the public baths with their feet in the steaming water playing draughts. The guards posted at the doors sweat inside their armour. The oarsmen are issued with new tunics on their way out. It is an improbable holiday.

There is delay. Ships come in all the time until the sea is an endless vista of vessels riding at anchor. Pity poor Carthage.

25

Clodia's grandmother is at her table by the tall window of her room sorting through her letters. The table top is hidden beneath them. There are piles of letters tied together with ribbon among the unsorted drifts. Some of the seals are old and darkened with age, the paper yellowed and thin. A life distilled into the remains of a correspondence. It is the work of her leave-taking, this reordering of the past, a last attempt to catch the melody, to hear the cadence behind the notes. The fine patrician cheekbones are lambent against the shadow.

Clodia is standing by the lighted lamps in the dark corner of the room like a naughty child. She speaks with her face to the wall.

'You know what he said to me? He said that he took the Republican view that the phenomenon of sexual union was given to man not as a source of pleasure but for the procreation of sons. The phenomenon of sexual union. He made it sound like a proposition in philosophy, not like... what it is.'

The old woman knows. There is a restlessness in the girl, some unmistakeable inner turbulence that bespeaks her new knowledge, her new condition. Cornelia says,

'What else did he say, your husband to be?'

'He said that I was not to be afraid, that he would respect me for my father's sake and honour me as a duty to the sacrament of marriage...'

She snorts with laughter, holding her hand over her mouth as if she were six.

'I bet he learned that from a book. I wanted to pinch him. They are all so... so... pompous.'

'When is it to be, the marriage?'

'I don't know. Nobody tells me. I'm only the bride. Sometimes I feel like a doll... an item of dry goods.'

She likes to use that expression – an item of dry goods. Her grandmother says,

'It is not the way you think.'

'What isn't?'

'Between men and women. They can do less than they think they can and we can do more than we think we can.'

The old woman continues to sort through the letters for a moment and then pauses with a letter open in her hand.

'During the war, when I was a girl, laws were passed by the men in the Senate forbidding women to wear coloured clothes or to ride in carriages. Except for wedding rings, gold jewellery was forbidden too. Sumptuary laws, they were called. It seemed to be the right thing then, during the war, with so many widows and orphans in the city. When the war was over, two or three years after – I was already a married woman and your uncle Cornelius was a baby – the women

96

of Rome campaigned to have the laws repealed. Old Cato was Consul then and he would have none of it. The Censors that year were both called Brutus, I remember.'

Cornelia shakes her head faintly in bemusement.

'Sometimes I remember such strange things. They pop into my mind like bubbles, things I didn't even know that I knew...... Where was I ?'

'The sumptuary laws.'

'In the end on a particular day the women of Rome simply took to the streets in their coloured dresses and their embroidered shawls and their jewellery that had lain at the bottoms of drawers through the war years and the better off women went out in their carriages. My mother came for me in her carriage and she made me put on a red dress and we drove down from the Palatine and into the Forum. The coachman was all of a dither. The place was packed with carriages full of women gorgeous as parakeets. She never seemed to be afraid, my mother. It was full of women, the Forum. It was like a carnival, so many colours...'

Cornelia has gone back to her reading, lost again among the invisible mirages of her past. Clodia is passing her hand above the flame of the oil lamp, across and back, across and back, so that streaks of lampblack crisscross her palm. The silence in the room lasts until Clodia says,

'And what happened? Did they change the law, the sumptuary law?'

She likes the sound of 'sumptuary.'

'The law? I don't know if they changed the law but I do know that the matter of coloured dresses and carriages and gold jewellery was never raised in our house after that. Mother seemed to make a point of appearing at her most flamboyant whenever father had guests in the house or whenever they were out together... but he never said a word. Cato is supposed to have said in the senate, "We rule the world, gentlemen, and our women rule us."'

In the gloom away from the window, the light flickers with the passage of the girl's hand above the flame. Cornelia's voice falls silent again as she reads. Clodia is watching her. The old woman smiles at the faded brown ink. She says absently,

'He never was much of a writer.'

97

'Who?'

'It was the sound of his voice.'

'Who?'

'I can hardly even picture him. I remember his voice, the smell of his body, the muscles in his neck.'

'Who?'

'Varro. It was when your grandfather was away with the army in Spain.'

'Who was he?'

'Varro? A charioteer. My first lover.'

The old woman reads on, apparently lost. Clodia's hand has halted in its path over the flame as she stares at the old woman. She pulls her hand away with a start. Out of the confusion of her thoughts she says,

'I had a letter from Aemilianus. He's in Sicily with the fleet.'

'Oh?'

'A place called Lilybaeum.'

26

On the beach by the town of Lilybaeum the schoolchildren are lined up. They have been given little flags to wave. The whole town is on the beach. The crowds are animated and the day has a carnival atmosphere. The shopkeepers and stallholders have closed up for the day and come down themselves to watch. The harbour quays have been closed to the public: officials and invited guests only. There are delegations and deputations from the chief towns of Sicily. The families of the Consuls and the senior officers who have travelled this far to bid a last farewell have been given chairs overlooking the slapping swells. A temporary altar has been set up and prayers are being offered up. The smell of incense comes and goes in the breeze.

The anchored ships of the invasion fleet are spread out as far as the eye can see in every direction. Two hundred ships they say: sixty thousand men.

A barber is standing next to a butcher on the beach. They are trying to count the number of ships they can see. The barber says,

'Me, I'm from Carthage, you know, originally. Came over here with my family when I was six. My dad set up in business here in Lilybaeum, barbering. He used to say there was too many barbers in Carthage. More barbers than you could shake a stick at, he used to say. So he come here. He's dead now, my dad and I'm still the only barber in town, well except for the bloke who works in the public baths. I've got relatives in Carthage, uncles and aunts and that. I must have a lot of cousins too. My mother used to keep in touch but she's been dead a long time. Being a bloke, I never bothered... And it's only a couple days on the ferry.'

The butcher says, 'A hundred and thirty two. I make it a hundred and thirty two.'

The barber continues,

'I can't remember hardly anything about Carthage. The woman who lived next door had a cat and we used to have a great big tank full of rainwater. Under the floor, it was. It used to frighten me, looking down into that black water when my mother lifted the lid. I used to dream about it. One of my uncles was called Kolo. At least that's what we called him, uncle Kolo. He was a barber too. He must be an old bloke now. Fat he was. I've got a lot of relatives in Carthage.'

The barber is gazing out at the ships.

'Poor buggers.'

'Who?'

'Who do you think? The Carthaginians. Don't fuck with the Romans.'

Half a mile away across the water from the barber and the butcher, on the crowded deck of the *Bellerophon* the chief priest is struggling to keep the contents of his stomach down. The chief priest is no sailor and the movement of the anchored ship in the passing swells is making him uneasy. Under his hands the bound goat convulses as he cuts the artery. The blood pumps vigorously into the bowl for a few moments and then more slowly. The goat's eyes grow filmy and it dies with a shudder. The chief priest slits open the body, reaches in for the hot entrails. From where he sits on his bench the playwright watches the chief priest struggling with his nausea. The prayers continue. Censorinus and Manilius the Consuls are standing bareheaded with members of the general staff, impassive through these required rituals. Another priest, a youth, an acolyte, takes the steaming tray of red and blue offal across the deck and at the appropriate pause in the prayer he hurls the contents out over the water but he is nervous and he loses his grip on the tray and the innards fall down between the oars. The playwright watches the glinting tray slice down, arcing back and forth like a falling leaf through the water, down and down into blue green oblivion. A loop of offal hangs over an oar. On the deck the chief priest loses his struggle and vomits helplessly into the bowl of blood. When he looks up again aghast, his grey green face is spotted with scarlet. Among the military there is a tightening of facial muscles. Manilius steps away, outraged by this farce, and bawls for the bosun. The windlass pawls chatter as the anchor comes up and as it clears the water the bosun brings the beater down on the stroke drum. The oars lift in unison. Signal flags go up the mast and everywhere on that wide sea the ships of the fleet are responding and the anchors are coming up.

Below the deck of the *Bellerophon* in the improvised Consular cabin, on a camp table which has been lashed to the ship's timbers, among the litter of maps and despatches and half eaten food lies a packet. The packet is flat, documents, and is tied with ordinary string and sealed with the heavy seal of the Roman Senate: SPQR. Hardened dribbles of red wax run across the corner below the heavy impress of the sealstone. Inside the packet lie the orders, the as yet unread orders of the Senate concerning the conduct of the war against the city of Carthage. It lies among the litter of papers, an unremarkable object. Above the cluttered table a cold lantern swings.

The packet weighs as much as a shoe maybe or a modest book of poems. You might think of this packet lying in this empty place as a kind of seed from which will grow a tree, a great tree of suffering, its boughs heavy with strange fruit. You might think too, in contemplating this mundane object, of the terrible determinations of the word.

The War

27

The army of Rome is encamped among the dunes outside the port of Utica. The delegation of elders has arrived from Carthage. They climb down from two tumbril-like carts in their long sackcloth shirts. There are twenty of them, dignitaries of the city, with oiled beards and long ringlets. They stand in the wide stony space with the wind driving skeins of sand against their legs so that it seems as if they are standing in some wide and racing river.

Manilius has had staging set up among the coastal dunes, a high rostrum with awnings and pennants. To left and right of this staging, as far as the eye can see stretch the formations of the Roman army. They are drawn up in parade ground order in their centuries and maniples, an undulating mile-long wall of sun reflecting steel. Above the heads of the troops straining banners dwindle toward infinity. Fifty yards in front of the high place where Manilius and his fellow Consul sit, a rope barrier has been set up in the sand so that the Carthaginians are kept at a distance, like lepers. This is a play or a pageant in which the subjection of one nation to another is being acted out. There is a certain familiarity with the protocols, the symbolic form, in the way that the delegation move up to the rope, for this is not so much an enactment as a re-enactment.

A week ago, from the same rostrum, in the presence of the same awesome host, Consul Censorinus (for Manilius has a speech impediment and is no public speaker) delivered the demands of the Senate and the Roman People to the same uneasy group of Carthaginian elders.

All weapons both public and private, all siege equipment, catapults, onagers, all ammunition for the same, all spears, shields, swords, bows, javelins, all slings, slingstones, armour, helmets, all cavalry equipment, all materials whatsoever for the prosecution of war are to be delivered up within forty eight hours of the issue of this edict to Marcus Manilius and Lucius Marcius Censorinus, Consuls.

The carts began leaving Carthage through the Utica Gate in the early morning following the return of the delegation. In his history of the war Appianus states that the vast column that left the city carried two thousand heavy catapults of all types together with weapons and armour for two hundred thousand men.

The giant bonfires made from these war materials are still burning behind the Carthaginian elders as they gather again behind their rope barrier. A black flag of smoke from these fires drifts out to sea, obscuring the anchored warships. They have complied to the letter with the demands of the Senate and the Roman People. Abasement is total, unquestioning. Opinions in Carthage vary about the next stage of the humiliation of the city, but everyone expects that it will be money, reparations, a heavy indemnity for breaking the terms of Africanus' treaty. What else could it be? What else can they want? Carthage is disarmed, helpless. She has willingly placed her neck beneath Rome's heel. What else can they want?

Censorinus stands and begins to speak. Not all of the Carthaginians speak Latin. The distance between the supplicants and the speaker is wide and the wind that is blowing off the sea carries the sound of Censorinus' voice away into the desert. There is some confusion and the Carthaginians are signalling for a written version of the speech. On the rostrum Censorinus is looking about in agitation, having come to the end of his prepared address and his aides are conferring. Finally two officers hurry across with a rolled document to the rope barrier and a huddle of Carthaginian elders begins to read. Censorinus begins his speech again.

Something is happening among the Carthaginians. One old man, a high priest, a senior member of the group, kneels on the ground and begins to pour handfuls of sand over his head. Another priest, a fat man with the long ringlets of his caste begins to wail like a hired mourner, a thin and carrying keening. Censorinus glances up uncertainly from his text. Another tears off his shirt and stands naked. He begins to scratch at his face and the flesh of his body so that the weals he raises are visible to the troops a hundred yards away. A little knot are still reading and rereading the text of the speech, gesturing and shouting and arguing. To the stolid ranks of Roman troops they look like madmen, crazed hermits, dervishes, as they roll about and wail and pour sand upon their heads and pluck at themselves.

Censorinus stops reading. There is a puzzled stillness among the aides and generals on the podium. They are oddly helpless in the face of this bizarre and frenzied demonstration and they wait in a kind of embarrassment until at last it seems to be over and the Carthaginians lie spent and still. At last they stand up again, the dignitaries, helping one another to their feet, dusting themselves off as best they can. After the strange drama it is all bathos, all foolishness, a sort of coming to, a return to the requirements of the moment.

According to Appianus' history of the war the central utterance in Censorinus' speech is to be understood as follows:

'Yield Carthage to us, and betake yourselves where you like, for we are resolved to raze your city to the ground.'

28

Spendios dips his pen into the ink and withdraws it with the unthinking turning motion of the professional scribe. He waits for the words to come, the pen poised. A drop of ink trembles from the nib to the blank page.

There are no words. I am so frightened. It is the fear of death. I am new to these things. I have seen things today I never thought to see.

He looks at what he has written. He dips the pen into the ink.

Across the street, outside his shop, Statius the cobbler is hanging from his own shop sign. His tongue is black. There are flies on his tongue and in his eyes. His eyes are open. He was Italian, not even a Roman. He came from the South of Italy. They say that all the Italians in the city have been killed. They hanged Statius this afternoon, after we heard the news.

The words flicker from the pen but they do not unlock the anguish. The ache of dread is a stone in his belly. He begins again.

We waited on the walls by the Utica gate for the return of the elders, thousands of us. Some had gone out to meet them as they approached the city so that by the time they passed through the gate beneath us they were hardly to be picked out in the mob. There was shouting and jostling but they would not speak and continued toward the parliament building like condemned men, with all the crowd behind them in a great press. I found myself behind the one they call Hannibal the Starling, an old man with sand in his hair. All I could see of him was the top of his head as he was borne along like a piece of frail flotsam. When we came up through the gates of the Byrsa to the parliament building itself the whole mass of us went through the huge double doors and into the senate chamber. I have never been in that place before. It was not built for the likes of me. It is a great circular place with benches for a large number of people. The members of the Council of a Hundred were sitting at the front like people on the front row at a circus, staring. The movement of the crowd faltered and stopped just inside the great doors of the council chamber. We were all suddenly abashed, like children who have stumbled by chance into some forbidden place, and for a moment nothing happened until the elders of the delegation began to move into the central space. We edged around the outer wall and watched as they shuffled forward in their sackcloth shirts like fugitives from a madhouse, dishevelled and staring. A silence fell, the strangest thing. I have never been so frightened as I was in the moments when old Hannibal the Starling moved to the podium. He unrolled a document and read out to us the decree of the Roman Senate in a voice that was no more than a trembling whisper. He did not move when he had finished speaking but just stood there gripping the podium with both hands as if he might fall, and the silence did not break. And then the senator who was standing right behind him stood up and picked up the bench he had been sitting on and moved up behind him with the bench held above him in both his hands. He brought it down on the back of the old man's head and the old man went down beneath it.

Spendios is living through the moments. For a long time he does not move at all, and then he begins to write again.

They killed them all, all of the members of the delegation, and when the place had emptied and the madness had gone out into the city I was still standing by the wall of that empty echoing hall. The corpses lay among the benches like lumps of bloody rag. A cat came and stood in the open doorway and then walked out again.

He stops writing. He is invaded by a strange lightness of being and he is not afraid. Fear falls away. He sits motionless in a new space that is for a precious moment unknown to dread.

A week later he writes,

War has been declared. The city gates are shut. Watchers have been posted on all the walls. It is days now since the Romans issued their edict and still they have not come. The city is an ant heap. There is work going on everywhere. There is scaffolding on the old citadel walls and there are labourers and slaves everywhere. Except that the slaves are not slaves any longer. They have been freed, all of them, by decree of the Council of a Hundred. It is a strange thing. Everything has changed for the slaves and nothing. They still work at the same tasks, eat the same food.
The streets are solid with carts. The temples are being opened up as workshops for the manufacture of weapons. The work is going on day and night. Two streets away in the Tanit Temple they are making swords. I lie in bed and listen to the sound of the hammers. They say that catapults are being built in the dockyards. Militia groups are being mobilised in each of the districts. I had to go to a meeting the other night in the temple at the bottom of the street and now I have a number – I am number one hundred and thirty seven – and they say we are to be issued with spears. Twice now we have been learning how to march in the open space behind the old bakery. Mostly we are balding, middle aged. The young men did not come

back from the war in the desert. It feels very strange. I never imagined myself as a soldier. So far we have marched with broom handles instead of spears.

There are militia companies in all of the city districts: Gapn, Ugar, Hubur, Qor-maym. The streets around the Byrsa have been subdivided. I am a member of Thitmanit, the eighth unit of the district. We are all from the same street. I have never thought of myself like that, as somebody who lives on a particular street.

Yesterday I held the ladder while Gisco the blacksmith and his son cut down the cobbler's body. I helped to push him on a handcart to the cemetery. His flesh was black and he smelt like a dead dog. A pair of my shoes still lies on his shelf, waiting to be collected. There was a crowd at the cemetery, a lot of women with their husbands. I think some of the men were the ones who had hanged him. The women had brought flowers and they sang a hymn. They sang Anat's Lament. It is an old song. I have heard arrangements of it at the opera. I was glad of the singing. It was a moving thing, a liberating thing. There was a lot of weeping. I wept myself, like a child. Standing next to me was Mara the widow with her head shaved and I clung on to her and wept. She seemed very strong and calm. It was in the middle of the afternoon. I was holding on to her and she was stroking my hair and I felt the swell of her breasts. These are new things for me. It is like being born again. This new world I have been born into fills me with dread, and yet, in my secret heart, I would not have it otherwise than it is.

I was out today trying to buy bread. A woman next to me in the queue said that she was going home to shave off her hair. She says that there is a shortage of rope for the new catapults and that the women are starting to send their hair to the rope works. I thought of Mara and of how strong she looked with her head shaved, like a man. I thought of the swell of her breasts.

They say that the Senate has sent word to fat Hasdrubal who fled the city last year. They sentenced him to death for losing the war against the Numidians but he escaped. They say that he has raised another army and that he had planned *to march on Carthage himself. The Senate, in their panic, have pardoned Hasdrubal. They have pleaded with him to defend his native city. They have begged him to give battle to the Romans. It seems to me that Hasdrubal's choice may determine our fate. If he chooses to place his army at Rome's disposal then our doom will not be long delayed.*

Mother seems hardly to notice. She sits on the balcony with her lacework.

29

The two rams stand like streets of houses a hundred yards apart on the wide beach facing the city wall. The great iron bound wheels are twice the height of a man. The rams themselves, made from pine trunks bound ten together by iron hoops, are colossal, a hundred feet long. They hang from lengths of anchor chain beneath the pitched roofs of the long carriages, primitive, malevolent, altogether too huge, too heavy. They brood under the sign of purpose, of brute unthinking intent, like emblems of Rome itself. The guards lounging in the shadow of these leviathans seem no more than a tiny flicker of insubstantial limbs.

The sun will rise in an hour. The soft air is the colour of pewter. Columns are moving up the shore from the camps. Gulls take off across the dim lagoon. Six thousand men have been allotted to each ram: the whole of the fourth legion to the one and the oarsmen from thirty warships to the other: the army versus the navy. They will bring the rams up to the walls of Carthage and pound them until they fall down. It is very simple.

They will work in shifts of two hours, a thousand men to a shift. An iron rail has been fixed along both sides of the ram itself and seventy men take up positions along each side. Ships' hawsers run out behind the rams and men line up like long tug of war teams to the rear. Squads with long levers are posted to each of the sixteen huge wheels. Artillery is moving up within range of the city walls ready to drive the defenders off when the rams are moved up. Preparations are unhurried. Teams with ladders and water pumps are moving along the length of the ram soaking the hides which are nailed to the pitched roof. Men stand about in their places waiting. The sun moves up the sky and shadows grow shorter. The day will be hot. On the walls of the city heads appear momentarily here and there above the parapet.

The playwright finds himself standing next to his African beneath the roof of the ram only yards back from the great iron hammerhead. It is cool in the shade of the dripping roof. To one side of him in the sunlight, dwarfed behind a wheel, men lean on their long levers talking and looking about. Four hundred yards to the rear the men of the tenth legion wait under arms to advance through the gap that the rams will create.

The fact that the city of Carthage is still standing is a continuing surprise, a kind of enigma. It is midsummer and the army of Rome has been in Africa since early spring. For weeks after the city was emptied of its armaments, by treachery in the opinion of some, men waited for the blow to fall. The Consuls were to be seen out and about with their aides. Maps and diagrams were drawn up, discussions held, plans made for the picking of this simple undefended cherry. At last the rumour came that the seventh legion was to attack the triple wall using ladders. Old soldiers sucked their teeth. The attack failed. The seventh legion did not even cross the first of the three huge walls. At the wall's foot the Roman columns came under a crushing deluge of stones. The tall ladders with their vertical burdens of heavy infantry were pushed sideways by the defenders, falling against each other like dominoes in a comic interlude of broken bones and crushed bodies. Greek fire burst among the milling thousands, hideous napalm. Twelve hundred dead. That night in their pavilions the Consuls contemplated a new future, a new landscape of the spirit. The broken legion was marched away to Utica to isolate the contagion of dismay. The dead were buried at night. Official despatches to Rome were economical with the truth.

The rams are the answer. Three months in the making, these engines will reduce the walls to rubble and the advancing legions will march into Carthage as along a highroad. The focus of the attack will be that stretch of the wall which runs to the south of the city between the triple wall and the harbour entrance. The wall is lower here, older, a single fragile veil of masonry. The legions will pour through the gaps and the unarmed citizens will melt away before the onslaught.

The attack develops mundanely. There are no drums, no trumpets. The playwright and his companions are ordered down from the ram housing and the wheel men begin to work the huge structures forward across the sand. The ponderous engines inch forward on twin roadbeds of timber. As the engines pass over, the split trunks are brought round from the rear and placed beneath the groaning wheels again. There is rivalry here and the navy are making better progress. The chanting of the oarsmen can be heard by fishermen out on the lagoon. The walls are empty. There is nothing of war in any of this termite activity, nothing except imminence. Thousands labour to bring this mystery to birth, as if it were something long portended. What the first day wrote the last day shall read. Shouted orders sound in the blank light. Backs bend. The rams crawl toward the vacant ramparts.

The ram of the oarsmen thumps to a halt against the wall and the playwright and his companions are ordered back beneath the housing. Each man finds a handhold on the iron rail that runs the length of the great hammer. In the rear the rope teams take up the heavy hawsers. The playwright's African spits into the calloused pink palms of his hands and winks deadpan. Ahead, framed by the timbers of the ram housing, the playwright can see a sunlit square of ancient masonry. There is a pause, a moment that gathers.

On the first word they brace their feet, re-establish their grip on the rail. On the second they swing the swaying hundred-ton piledriver back on its chains. On the third they drive it forward with a roar. Reverberation stuns. The shock runs up the playwright's arms. His ears ring.

The ram comes back again, slowly, stops, drives forward. Waves of concussing vibration wash back down the gallery. Men clasp their hands under their armpits and cry out.

The ram comes back, slowly. Fifty yards to the left the ram which is manned by the fourth legion delivers its first blow with a sound that the playwright will remember as pain in the cavity of his chest and then he is carried forward like a rag doll as he clutches the iron rail and is stunned again.

Above his head comes the sound of heavy rain. It is liquid phosphorous, Greek fire, thundering down from the wall above to the hide roof and cascading to the sand in a flaming downpour. Men recoil from the shrivelling heat. Out on the sand a doused NCO is a screaming torch. The roof of the ram steams and hisses and scalding water drips through the hides on to the men below. A storm of artillery fire passes overhead. Onager stones shatter against the stone rampart and flights of catapult bolts deflect from the battlement in ringing showers of sparks. An onager stone rebounds from the upper wall and crashes through the roof of the ram, killing an oarsman and breaking the legs of another. Spots of blood run in a wavering line along the dust-white timber as the weeping man is carried back along the length of the ram housing. The playwright is aware of a momentary glint of scarlet by his own foot. The ram housing is a confused vista of heat and noise.

Madness kindles like fire and the oarsmen commit their bodies in blind rage to the numbing work. The small square of white masonry, half lost in a trembling haze of dust and smoke, which is all that can be seen of the city of Carthage by the men inside the ram, is the target, the focus, the simple, primitive and absolute goal. They work to the song of the oar.

O Opop!

O Opop!

O Opop!

To fishermen out on the lagoon the thump of the distant rams sounds across the water like the world's faltering heartbeat. The pulverised craters in the city wall grow deeper. Sudden fissures race upward to the wall top and choking dust fills the long gallery of the ram. The oarsmen are possessed by the task, blind and deaf to all but the dim square of stone. The knuckled and riveted head of the ram slams home like the hammer of god.

Squalls of burning rain drive across the roof above them unnoticed and the din of artillery is no sound at all. They exist only in the stunned, sweating, deafened aftermath of the ram's impact.

A slippage in the stone square, a jerky derangement of the coursed masonry and the vertical wall falters from the true, transmutes fantastically into a liquid deluge of dissolving stone. Monstrous blocks bounce away in the fog of smoke and dust. The front of the ram fills with a roaring avalanche of stone. Men at the front are crushed to death, buried. The simple square of impenetrable masonry has shrunk to a horizontal slit of light, a lunar vista of rubble stretching back into a smoking and palpable distance. The playwright stands deafened and blank and sick with his back bent and his hands on his knees. His breath rasps hoarsely in and out, in and out.

There is no pause. Passing either side of the ram are the men of the tenth legion advancing under their packs. They pass along below the panting oarsmen at a stolid run and begin to climb the great cone of the destroyed wall to the beat of the drum, like robots, like warriors grown from dragons' teeth. Centurions curse them and whip them on with their swagger sticks as if they were animals, mules. They pass up the steep scree slope between hanging walls to left and right and are seen for a moment at the summit against the light before they pass down into the city.

The African, dust white, pulls the playwright down from his place and together they toil up the slope among the grunting legionaries. At the summit they stop, kneeling among broken stones, and the mules pass on down the slope. What the playwright sees is a vision, a dream.

There is no highroad into the city, no broad avenue of conquest. What he sees, facing him forty yards away, is a wall of tenements, six, seven stories high. It is a poor part of town. He can see washing hanging from the balconies of these cliffs of peeling limewash. The narrow alleys that run back into the darkness are impassable, blocked and barricaded with timber, rubbish, anything. At every one of a hundred windows, on every floor, on the rooftops, there are people, crowds of them, faces indistinguishable, and they are throwing stones down, bricks and stones. Below them the tenth legion is dying under this downpour. The men of the legion are coming down the slope, sliding and stumbling under the weight of their equipment, century after century, into the cauldron. There is no exit from the cauldron. They are packed together, more every minute, and the killing stones are raining down upon them.

There is something banal in this, something of the everyday. It is simply a plan gone wrong, a miscalculation. Who was to know that there was no road, no city street passing between these tenements? Death comes stupidly under the numb deluge.

A shoulder crushed and ruined by a brick thrown by a ten year old from the rooftop a hundred feet above. Death follows in a few days.

A skull crushed inside a deformed helmet by a shard of paving stone, blood running from both ears. Death follows within minutes.

A foot smashed flat by a block of masonry. Death within a month from gangrene.

They mill in their thousands enduring the dreadful matter-of-fact destruction of their bodies, crushed together like the surging crowd at the games.

The playwright and the African watch from the summit of the white hill, bearing the necessary witness to these things.

30

The sound of the rams comes up through the surface of the street itself, fills the narrow canyon with its profound double heartbeat. The members of Thitmanit militia hurry toward the sound, threading the narrow streets, shouldering through the tide of people that is flowing against them. Spendios' heart is beating high under his ribs like a bird as he pushes between the tight-faced mothers and the wailing infants. Ahead of him the column slows and he comes up against the baker's back. The fat man turns and gives him the blank uncomprehending look of a drowning man. The scribe sees Mara the widow dip the shaft of her spear as she ducks into a doorway and a moment later he too is stumbling in the sudden dark of a rank tenement hallway. They go up the flights of wooden stairs and the stairwell thunders like the sea with the sound of their feet while beneath the roaring the basso profundo note of the ram tolls out of the abyss. Open doors give off the landings into rooms where armed men and women are demolishing the window casements. Men are clumping down from the roof carrying piles of bricks.

Five, six flights of stairs and Spendios is gasping as he comes up squinting to the broad light of the rooftop. The flat roof of the tenement is a demolition site. Everywhere there are people carrying bricks away or breaking up the capstones of the parapet with hammers and levering out the crumbling brickwork beneath. Teams are prizing out the flagstones of the flat rooftop and breaking them up. A line of washing hangs untouched across the space and people duck beneath the shirts as they move about. Thitmanit has been posted to the roof itself and the men and women are given places behind the parapet that overlooks the city wall. Spendios puts his hand on the flat top of the low parapet and feels the tremor of the ram's impact. The sound concusses. He looks down the cliff of stone to the cobbled square below, where scurrying figures are moving about. At the far side of the square rises the back of the city wall. It is still standing and he can see figures crouched behind the stone battlement. A flight of catapult bolts deflect from the wall top in a shower of sparks and they go whining over the scribe's head. He has no idea what they are. With each invisible blow of the ram the city wall blurs for an instant. Vision is scarfed. Stones jump out of the masonry and white dust pulses out of the jointing.

Next to him Mara is working the blade of her spear into the mortar between the bricks of the parapet in front of her. He takes her by the shoulder and points and for a moment she cannot understand. The city wall is moving. The solid cliff of stone is turning into a slow cataract, dissolving downward as in a dream, over and over. They watch together as the roaring vision loses itself behind rolling clouds of white dust.

The sound of the ram has ceased and as the last bouncing stone comes to rest, a blank white silence ensues. Dust drifts. Out of this slow fog looms a white hill. It rises in a smoking cone between broken ramparts. At the very summit, out of bleached obscurity, a man appears and stands for a moment alone as at the beginning of the world. It is a moment. Behind him come the mules, implacable, without number.

Spendios and the widow watch like spectators at the games as the attack develops below them. The Romans come down the slope and cross the square at a run, making for the entrances to the narrow alleys that run between the tenement blocks, but the alleys

114

are barricaded to the height of a man. As the Romans begin to pull away the piled debris, the timber, the broken carts and furniture, smoke begins to creep. The defenders are setting fire to the barricades. Romans are sliding down into the square all the time and the space is becoming congested, packed. There is no exit from this place.

They watch from the roof top as the first bricks and stones begin to arc out of the windows below them toward the dense mass below, like the first heavy drops of a downpour. On the roof they turn with sudden urgency to their work, he and she, together. The mortar is old between the bricks of the low wall and the heavy capstone begins to move. They lever it forward inch by inch until it topples into the void. They watch it go, turning over and over.

31

Consul Manilius sits at his desk in the night time silence of his tent composing the despatch which he is bound by law to send to the Senate in Rome each week regarding the conduct and progress of the war. The page before him is blank, the pen forgotten in his hand. He has just lost four thousand men. The Tenth Legion is ruined. At the roll call following the attack less than half of the men answered. The casualty stations are overwhelmed. Injuries are hideous, bodies broken and crushed in ways you could not even imagine. The sound of suffering is the cacophony of the zoo. He forced himself to make the tour of the dressing stations in the hours after the attack and now his mind makes him a stranger to himself. He sits at his desk wandering among the horrors, lost.

This was not how it was supposed to be. He did not bribe his way to the consulship for this. How smugly ecstatic he had been when his appointment was announced in the Senate. His place in history was guaranteed. His name would be remembered forever: Marcus Pleminius Manilius, the commander who led Rome to final victory over the Evil Empire: and he would make himself rich in the process. Oh, what a masterstroke it had seemed to him then. In those days everyone knew that Carthage was an overripe fruit, ready to fall. Everyone was wrong. Manilius winces at his own folly. Panic surges in his chest.

He knows because he has been told, that the Carthaginians are rebuilding the breaches in the city wall. They are working through the night, these ant citizens, by the light of torches, to secure their city again. For Manilius it is all a bad dream, a dream of impotent futility. Ruin stares him in the face. The Consul sits immobile, a vessel full of horror. Outside his pavilion, at this dead of night, burial parties are about their work.

32

Spendios lifts the latch and opens the door into the sunlit yard. The widow does not see him. She is washing clothes. She performs the task with the same matter-of-fact absorption that she throws bricks. He notices for the first time that her hair has grown back a little on her shaven head and his eye is caught by the tendons that run in her neck as she kneads her laundry. He does not know why he is here. He has no reason to be here that has a name and when she notices him he will have nothing to say. He will stand there foolishly holding the latch of her gate with nothing to say.

The widow pulls a dripping sheet from the water, folding it wetly upon itself as it comes clear of the washtub. She straightens her back and the shadowed world between her hanging breasts is lost to his gaze. Her eyes close in private voluptuous relief as she raises her shoulder blades and turns her neck, easing the ache in her back.

She opens her eyes and sees him. There is no surprise, no change of expression. She does not smile, only letting the sheet fold back slowly into the tub. The front of her dress is wet, dark and glistening. Spendios is looking at the front of her dress, at the jutting concentric circles of her nipples beneath the wet cotton. He is rapt, too new to what he feels to dissemble. He does not smile or speak but stares like a boy, mesmerised, unaware of himself, unaware of how ridiculous he might seem, how callow and unschooled. In his wordless, consumed fixity he does not think to speak.

As if it were the only possible resolution, the only imaginable next thing to happen, her hands move up to the buttons at the front of her shapeless dress. She lowers her head a little as she works the first button through the wet fabric. Her hands move down from button to button. Her fingers work the buttons free one by one and the dress gapes a little wider with each one. He experiences the glimpsed darkness of her groin. With a movement of her shoulders she shrugs the garment from her body and it falls in stiff folds around her ankles. She raises her head and looks at him as he stands with his hand on the latch.

33

Rome. The banquet is a private affair. It is being held in honour of Consul Mancinus who is back in Rome after two years as commander-in-chief of the army in Africa. It is two years since Mancinus replaced Manilius as commander in chief. Manilius was not much use, lost two legions they say, but Mancinus is a feckless fool, a patrician halfwit. They say that without young Tribune Aemilianus the war would have gone to the dogs entirely. Public opinion in the city is against the Consul. Almost three years and Carthage still stands. Disarmed and helpless, the city should have been in ashes within weeks. Rome is full of armchair generals whose only shared opinion is that Mancinus must go.

The Consul has been in the Forum all day standing in front of a large map of the city of Carthage, attempting to defend his reputation. He has a slight speech impediment which becomes pronounced when he is under pressure. Aemilianus' people arranged to have him heckled and he has had a difficult day. They have been putting it about that Carthage will only fall when Aemilianus assumes command of the besieging army. They have made of this assertion a kind of prophecy and the idea has taken hold among the plebs. Technically, Aemilianus, at twenty-seven, is too young for the Consulate but Quintus Fulvius Nobilior says there are precedents, there are precedents. The thing is possible.

Quintus Fulvius Nobilior is a tall man, lanky and big boned. He has broken veins in his nose. He is no orator and he has learned from experience to pursue his ends by other means. He is owed money in many quarters and this is an asset, politically speaking. It was Nobilior's debtors who were heckling Consul Mancinus today, though he will go with his new wife to the banquet which is to be held in the Consul's honour. Appearances are everything.

The banquet for the Consul will be Clodia's first public appearance as a married woman and though in her secret heart she loathes the pompous world of men and lives in a state of silent rebellion, and though their braying and bragging remain a mystery to her and she thinks of them as another species, hippopotami or crocodiles, she is beguiled by the idea of the banquet despite herself.

Old Cornelia sits by the window as her granddaughter parades up and down in a succession of expensive dresses. The floor is carpeted with abandoned garments. Clodia turns with a flourish and her crimson silk hems swish audibly across the mosaic. She grasps the full skirt in both hands and dances a few steps like a Spanish gypsy, her head over her shoulder. She says to her grandmother,

'What about this one? It's almost worth being married just so that you don't have to wear white all the time.'

'The red suits you. I have a ruby on a chain somewhere. Your grandfather gave it to me as a wedding present. It belonged to an African queen he said. She was called Sophonisba. She drank from a poisoned cup and died.'

Clodia stands on one leg in front of the mirror.

'Nobilior gave me a distaff on our wedding day, and a bound copy of the Twelve Tables. He takes the republican view about most things, not just the phenomenon of sexual union.'

She snorts with laughter as she studies the long mirror, watching herself uncertainly in the burnished copper as she moves this way and that to make the hems swish. She pictures herself lying beneath Nobilior with her eyes closed as he does his republican duty. Behind her eyelids she keeps the corded muscles in the playwright's neck, his sunburnt skin and the heat of his dissolving gaze. She keeps Hannibal the butcher of Carthage in that same darkness. She steps out of the dress disconsolately and stands naked, angular and matter-of-fact. She moves about grumpily lifting the scattered dresses with her toe.

'Not that one. Oh, I don't know. You choose.'

The long opulent room is a murmuring vista. Clodia stands silently behind her husband wearing her grandmother's ruby around her neck, watching the people. The men stand about like statues in their starched togas with their pomaded hair brushed forward in the antique manner. Men in togas never seem to move their necks she has noticed. They turn their whole bodies as if they were all suffering from stiff necks. The wives and society whores stand at their shoulders like highly coloured birds.

Mancinus' brother Velius is the host, a languid, slightly theatrical presence. He stands by his brother within the gilded doors with his sullen catamite, curling his fingers idly in the youth's ringlets as he welcomes the guests. Clodia feels her husband's disapproval of this Greek degeneracy like a cold draught. The boy has shaved off his eyebrows, Clodia sees, and painted on new ones so that the expression on his unblemished face is one of pained surprise. Consul Mancinus stands with his brother giving off bogus bonhomie. Behind the fixed smile is resentment and fatigue.

Nobilior is moving into the room and Clodia stays at her husband's elbow in the proper way as he scans the gathering, plotting his social itinerary. She is introduced to a fat senator, a piggy individual with dense hair growing from his nostrils and ears and she smiles through the tired innuendo which is her social portion as a new bride and is relieved when she becomes invisible again. Her husband and the fat senator fall into deep and important talk. The senator's female companion rolls her eyes for Clodia's benefit. She is tall and statuesque with an ample, white and perfumed cleavage. She has two painted beauty spots, one on the slope of her left breast and the other on her nose, which strikes Clodia as slightly odd. She says in a sort of stage whisper with the outstretched fingers of her bejewelled hand across her bosom,

'Tutilina.'

'Clodia Aemilianus.'

'Oh I know who you are. And how is it?'

The question takes in the whole phenomenon of marriage in general and the tribulations of the newly married in particular. Clodia thinks for a moment.

'I should say that it was very… er… very republican.'

Tutilina's eyes widen and she stifles a shriek of laughter. She takes Clodia by the arm and whispers conspiratorially,

'Come on. I shall turn to a pillar of salt if I have to listen to any more of their nonsense. Let's go and find someone interesting.'

Lucius Ambivus Turpio is an actor manager, a short man, a parodic thespian with thin red hair going to pink and a florid complexion. He breaks off in mid sentence as Tutilina arrives on the fringes of his circle with Clodia in tow.

'Darling! Darling! What a surprise. What a delight. My dear.'

He takes Tutilina by the hands and holds her at arms length. She is a head taller than he and he gazes up in admiration.

'Still as beautiful as ever. The best Queen Dido on the Aventine. She used to work for me, you know, this one…'

Turpio addresses himself to Clodia with camp familiarity.

'…until she found an easier living…'

He raises an arch eyebrow at the girl.

'…whilst I, on the other hand, have remained true to the muse, a victim on the altar of Art… Do you know, I was performing tonight, tonight, can you imagine, before I came here. Hardly had time to take off the paint. Terentius' *The Eunuch*. I play Dorus, the eunuch. It's about all I'm good for these days…'

Tutilina shrieks.

'…but I am being rude. Tutilina my dear you must introduce me to your charming protégé.'

'This is Clodia Aemilianus, the sister of Scipio Aemilianus.'

Turpio affects comical consternation and performs an exaggerated courtesy. He says with a twinkle of mockery in his eye,

'You must forgive me. I am unused to such exalted company, being but a poor player. Are you a theatre goer, Clodia Aemilianus?'

'Yes. Yes, I am. At least I would like to be. I saw you once in Caecilius' *The Brothers*. I thought you were very good.'

'Why thank you. A discerning critic, obviously, though to be frank I didn't always have such good fortune with his plays. In the early days we used to get hissed off the stage. Have you seen anything more up to the minute?'

'No, not really. My family are of the opinion that it's not patriotic to go to the theatre when there's a war on. The last thing I saw was *The General*.'

There is a silence. The play was only ever performed once. The author was condemned to the games. Turpio thinks he is being warned, that this is some display of aristocratic contempt. Clodia sees her mistake instantly.

'No, no. I liked it. I thought it was very funny. And clever.'

Turpio is wary. His gaiety has evaporated. He is trying to speak carefully.

'The play was well written, and you are right, it was funny too. But it is a foolish author who takes aim at the rich. Naevius was jailed a few years ago for mocking the members of the Senate and then they exiled him, but this... this. They had him killed you know... for writing a play. They had him butchered in the arena...'

Turpio falters. He wants to continue but he is lost for words. Clodia is shaking her head as if to drown the sound of his voice.

'No. He survived. He's in Carthage.'

Turpio is looking at the girl with his mouth half-open. At the far end of the room the double doors have opened and a fanfare of trumpets sounds painfully in the enclosed space. Four slaves move down the crowded salon carrying a sort of table at shoulder height. Mancinus and his brother have moved into the centre of the room and the slaves put down their burden. On the table is what looks like a cake, a great misshapen cake. It looks like an anvil or the head of an arrow, higher at one end. The cake sits in a sea of blue icing. There are little marzipan ships on the blue icing and little white marzipan houses and green marzipan trees on the cake itself. There are barleysugar temples and palaces made of candied fruit. Conversations have faltered and the guests stand about in puzzled anticipation. No one has made the connection. There is an exchanging of glances and the moment is in danger of becoming ridiculous, and then a foppish voice at the back says,

'I say, damned clever, what. It's Carthage. It's a Carthage cake.'

The penny drops among the armchair generals and there is a sudden enthusiastic babble. 'Look, that's the Byrsa, and look, that's the triple wall. There's the two harbours. How clever. That's the lagoon, there.' There is a scatter of applause as Mancinus' brother comes forward with a gilt tray on which lies an elaborate golden knife. He offers the knife on its tray to those nearest and the piggy senator with the nasal hair takes it up.

The senator is not quite sober and he wields the knife unsteadily, tearing untidy gashes through the city walls. He pulls out a great wedge of the cake and holds it up like a trophy above his head to noisy applause. Someone else takes up the knife, plunging it like a dagger into the Byrsa citadel and dragging the blade out through the streets to the sea. A hand reaches in and breaks off the twin lighthouses at the harbour entrance. Someone scoops up a handful of marzipan palm trees from the suburbs and flings them upward so that the fragments fall on the people standing near. There is laughter and shouting. The knife passes from hand to hand and the city is cruelly ploughed. Fingers claw the ground, rip up the temples and the houses and hurl them into the air. The togas are chanting and stamping.

34

August. Carthage bakes. The tall willow herb that has grown up everywhere between the flags of the half derelict inner harbour, has flowered and gone to seed. Skeins of soft seed-down lift in languid loops, drift and turn across the mirror of the harbour. Butterflies dance in the shimmering heat that rises from the red rusted iron chain hanging across the harbour mouth above its own inverted image.

These are the dog days of hunger, the days of blank imminence. The attacks of the previous summer against the city's defences are a memory and the cataclysm to come still lies behind the veil. Spendios moves along the rampart of the sea wall in his broad brimmed hat, his black shadow a moving circle on the hot stones.

To his right, seed floss drifts across the empty waters of the harbour, once solid with the world's shipping – drifts and turns. To his left, at the other side of the harbour wall, the sea breathes faintly and the distant ships of the blockade seem to hang just above the vague horizon, black specks, elusive as motes in the eye. Below him the waterfront is empty of shipping. It is a vista of broken masonry and abandonment where once ships were moored three deep as far as the eye could see, and the waterfront was busy day and night. Ships came over the horizon from the remotest corners of the world to Carthage.

Now nothing moves. The artery has been cut. No ships arrive in Carthage: none leave. The last of the blockade runners are gone, sunk by the rams of Roman warships or gone where the pickings are easier. Even the local fishermen avoid the city, selling their catches in the Roman camps along the shore. Up the coast the port of Utica thrives. Fifty yards out from the quay the mast and the sternpost of a sunken warship rise above their own coiled reflections.

It comes to him that this city, this other city disfigured by war and hunger, is his home. That city where he used to live lies in another country, that city of thoughtless cosmopolitan ease, that bustling untroubled hive.

The library in which he spent half his life is now the city granary where what remains of the grain reserves are piled in mounds around the walls of the great circular space, burying the books on their shelves. Dusty volumes can be glimpsed, still on their shelves, above the hills of millet. The labyrinth of scribes' desks is gone. Motionless queues of the starving stretch across the floor where the rows of desks once stood, and out through the tall doorway where bronze doors used to hang. Hasdrubal's thugs stand about with their long batons. Spendios goes there sometimes to help with the collection of Thitmanit's weekly ration of corn and he is unmoved, untouched by the strangeness of the time.

He does not regret the passing of that life and in his secret heart he would not choose it again. He is the willing servant of the war. It has borne him up, bestowed unexpected gifts upon him. It bestowed the gift of the widow upon him. He still goes to her house and they eat meagre meals together. He unbuttons her dress and closes his eyes against her breasts and she strokes his thinning hair and he finds only comfort there where once he discovered the fire in the blood. Starvation robs these things of their urgency.

The war has bestowed the gift of speech. He speaks to stallholders, barbers, butchers, apothecaries, plasterers, mosaicists, people who have lived in his neighbourhood for years, half-familiar, yet never spoken to in that city of the past. Since the war began they speak to him too, by his name, and it sometimes occurs to him that the hunger and the abiding sense of foreboding is a small price to have paid for this new belonging, this condition of being spoken to by name. In all his years at the library he never penetrated the polite, neutrally social surface, never discovered solitude's exit, but here among the emaciated men of his district it is all grossness, gallows' wit and unthinking acceptance. In some speechless place he is borne up by this inclusion, suffused by it, redeemed.

He sits around the brazier in the paling of the dawn with these unshaven, coarse individuals and he has his place there. The barber has brought a bottle of wine. There is no decent wine to be had. He makes this stuff from mildewed currants. The bottle passes from hand to hand as they stare in silence into the dying glow of the fire. When it comes to him the apothecary waves the bottle away.

'I have given up alcohol. It interferes with my suffering.'

They consider this. The barber says,

'Suffering is overrated.'

He comes to the end of the harbour wall, to the high bastion that juts out like a battleship above the deepwater harbour entrance with its rusting chain barrier and its dereliction of sunken shipping. Below him on the seaward side the quay broadens into a great square space, the choma, where the men of his militia troop lounge or doze beneath makeshift awnings amid the litter and ruin of war.

He sits in the shade of the rampart to be out of the sun. These days he needs to sit down often. He has eaten so little for so long. Beyond the harbour mouth to the South stretches the broad sand spit that divides the sea from the lake. He used to walk along its white sands sometimes, on his days off, before the war, in that other city. An empty place it used to be, save for the little wading birds that ran about in the lapping wavelets and the occasional fishing boat drawn up to be scraped and repainted. He remembers, in the black noon shadow of a fishing boat, lovers, pale urgent bodies, troubling, unforgettable.

The beaches are no longer empty. As far as the eye can see stretch the encampments of Rome. It is a vast place, a diminishing chequerboard of entrenched tented camps. In the spaces between the camps are scattered the materials and the debris of invasion: piles of timber, catapults, onagers, vehicles of every type drawn up in ragged rows, piles of rubbish, fires. Boats move out and back from the shore unloading the big transports moored in the offing. An endless line of troop ships drawn up on the sand diminishes along the littoral, loses itself in the heat haze. And everywhere there is movement, slight, ceaseless, purposeful: camel trains, carts, columns of infantry, prisoners. Men, uncountable thousands. It is a creeping of the world's skin. Spendios looks away.

The wide summit of the bastion where he sits is a rubbish tip. There are mounds of rubble and broken masonry everywhere. The battery of onagers, huge stone throwers hastily built and mounted here in the early days of the war, is skeletal wreckage The ancient wooden lighthouse that stood up here through the years of peace is a sprawled ruin. Round artillery stones as heavy as a man lie everywhere. A monstrous boulder launched months ago from the belly of a Roman catapult barge is embedded like a fallen meteor in its circle of shattered paving. Close by him a baulk of rotten timber lies in the heat. Out of its fissured papery surfaces insects boil, newly hatched flying ants. They mill about in their thousands, hop a little, once, twice, wings half extended, and then off, up, obliquely toward the sun, pilgrims, warriors of the light. They stream away like skeins of smoke toward the unbearable glare.

Spendios looks out again across the harbour mouth to the wide beaches where the termite army of Rome labours. A few hundred yards off, beyond the range of the catapults, rows of half built siege towers crepitate with labouring men. They grow taller by the day, these rolling towers. Faint sounds come to him through the afternoon shimmer. Rumour says that the Romans are planning a great causeway, a barrier, across the deep-water channel that will seal off the harbour entrance, and that these towers will be dragged across. He watches through the swift ant smoke.

There is some metaphor here, he knows, in these ant worlds, some trope, some comparative trick of the language suggestive of an answer, an explanation for what is happening, a truth. But that taste for the literary, the poetic is long gone from him. Writing is a foreign country to him now, a place he used to know but where he wanders now as a stranger. He writes his journal still, but it is a numb observance, a ritual without meaning. He likes to sit at his desk in the square of sunshine. He likes to do what is familiar. The writing itself is empty, runic, marks on a page, meaningless. Language no longer seems to him even to achieve the status of untruth. Speech has changed places with silence, has become inaudible to the act, to the life of the body, is merely a derangement, a troubling veil that is burst and shredded and annihilated by action, by panic and murder, by the beating of the heart and the pain of hunger in the belly, by the gross necessities of the body, by very breath. And even inaction, inert foreboding, even that shadow of the act to come seems to him to fall across the written page so that utterance passes over into blatter, into formless scrawl.

He stands up, moving about among the debris and finds a rusting length of iron bar beneath a broken onager, and returns to the seething ants. He composes himself for a moment for the acting out of this private mystery before he brings the heavy cudgel down with all his strength on the spongy wood. The rotten timber bursts into fragments and a million souls stream toward the sun.

35

Qart pulls his horse to a stop on the bare outcrop and his troop of Berbers clatter to a halt behind him. The dust raised by the horses' hooves continues forward so that they are momentarily enveloped in a fog of dust. The horses are breathing hard. Raised veins run beneath the sweating skin and white green froth gathers at the corners of their mouths where the bits pull. Horses and men are the colour of the dust. Effigies.

Below him the valley seems empty. He can just make out the distant line of bullock carts creeping through the afternoon shadows of cypress trees. He can see a detachment of cavalry at the head of the column. At the rear, hard to see among the cypress shadows there are more horse soldiers.

Times have changed. In the early days of the war these Roman supply convoys moved unescorted and made easy pickings. Camel caravans and transport columns came out of the South as if they were passing through the townlands of Rome itself, with no escort and no thought for the fate about to descend upon them. It was a game in those days. His stone-faced Berbers would kill enough of the camel drivers to convince them of the virtues of compliance. Sometimes the very sight of them, these veiled apparitions, was enough. They would drive the captured convoy to the nearest town on the coast and sell the whole affair to the highest bidder. Local fishing boats would take the goods up the coast for sale in Carthage. There was no blockade in those days. The Roman Consuls, civilian generals, were slow to learn. It was altogether a lucrative and sensible way to wage war. In those early days it was the Roman army that starved. Your Roman Consul was considered to be a dull witted creature by the men of Hasdrubal's army: slow on the uptake, a civilian, a know-nothing. You could carve a better general out of a banana. Hasdrubal ran the besieging army ragged.

Since Aemilianus' return from Rome with his new army, things have changed. The men of the Roman army no longer starve. Supplies are brought across the sea from Rome itself while Aemilianus makes Africa into a wasteland. He has tackled the source of his problem. By the logically impeccable device of destroying all food supplies in Africa whatsoever he has thereby ensured that none reaches the city of Carthage. Fields and villages for a hundred miles around the city have been burned and the livestock driven off or slaughtered. Farmers are butchered and their bodies dumped down wells along with the carcasses of their livestock. The refugee columns stretch from horizon to horizon. Africa is emptying. It is a blighted land, a land of ill omen, the wasteland.

For a year since Aemilianus returned like an angel of death the Roman fleet have been burning the coastal towns and exterminating the inhabitants. The least inlet village from which supplies might reach the city is destroyed. From beneath black palls of smoke the populations of the towns are marched out with their hands on their heads. These are very ordinary affairs, these destructions. There is seldom any resistance. The people are rounded up and marched out with their hands on their heads while the ghetto burns behind them.

Taking only six weeks, the men of the Fourth Legion built a fortified camp across the whole isthmus facing the triple wall of the city. This camp stretches from one lake to the other, cutting off the land route to Carthage. It takes a bold and canny smuggler to reach the city at all. The heads of those not quite bold or canny enough can be seen on poles on the ramparts of the camps. Their blackened and crucified corpses hang against the sky.

The blockading warships have sunk or frightened off all but the hardiest skippers. With an onshore wind a fast trader can still make it through the war galleys to the safety of the walled harbour but few are inclined, despite the money that can be made. The survivors of a rammed blockade runner are always shot to death in the water. In the ports of the inland sea, in the taverns and bordellos where sailors are to be found, the name of Carthage is seldom uttered. It is a bad luck name. 'That place,' they will say.

These days the Roman army is eating well. It is Carthage that starves. Hasdrubal has been outfoxed. Soon he will take his hungry infantry battalions within the city walls and only the cavalry squadrons will remain outside to harass the Roman supply lines. They live in the saddle, these horsemen, Berbers, Numidians, untribed men, no better than brigands. Hasdrubal has thrown them to the dogs. It is no longer clear to them who is the hunter and who the hunted. Losses are heavy. They ride under the banner of Phameas the prince. Phameas is a son of old Masinissa, born on the wrong side of the blanket. He has worked hard for Carthage, he and his horsemen, these three years. His sister lives in Carthage with her Carthaginian husband and her children. Phameas loves his sister well and so with the straightforward logic of his love he has been working hard to keep the Romans out of that city. But the time is drawing to a close. This is the endgame. Phameas has called the captains together.

Qart watches the last of the Roman cavalry emerge into the open valley bottom: four maybe five hundred men. At his own back there are eighty. He pulls his horse around.

Phameas sits in the saddle with a straight back. He is a man in his prime, a strong man. He has an open heart and no one speaks against him. His word is trusted. He has taken no part in the squabbles following Masinissa's death for it does not occur to him to make any claim on the dead king's legacy. As he says, he is only one of the old man's many bastards and it is understood that a bastard should have no expectations in these cases. He fights for pay against the Romans and for his good name and for the love of his sister and her children.

He has ridden out beyond the campfires across the level salt flats in the half dark of evening with his captains cantering behind him. He reins in his horse and waits. He motions them in so that he does not have to shout to be heard. The distant campfires flicker like planets in a level line. He begins to speak and it is clear to Qart that he has thought carefully about what he will say. Qart admires his honesty, his lack of guile. Phameas says,

'We have been fighting this war for three years and it is now my opinion that it cannot be won. Carthage has no friends left in the world. I believe that whatever we do now, the city will fall. The few thousand cavalry which we command cannot alter that. The Roman Aemilianus has sent word to me that he will welcome anyone who so desires into the service of Rome. Tonight I shall ride with the men who are under my direct command to Aemilianus' camp outside Carthage. I have brought you out here away from the men so that you may choose freely in this matter.'

Phameas pauses in his speech. In the darkness he cannot read his officers clearly, cannot quite catch the feeling. He anticipates the question.

'I trust him. I believe him to be a man of his word. He will not betray us I think. And now, if you are going to ride with me to Carthage go now and speak to your men so that they too can decide. We must leave soon.'

By ones and twos the dark shapes of the horsemen turn and urge their horses back toward the fires. The cantering hooves drum to silence across the salt levels. Phameas sits and watches them go. Only one other rider remains. Qart says,

'It is the right thing. Everyone knows. Do not judge yourself.'

'But not you.'

'Not me. Take my men with you tonight. I will speak to them.'

'Where will you go?'

'To Carthage'.

36

The city of Carthage has two walls enclosing it. The inner wall, the ancient citadel wall, protects Dido's city – the Byrsa hill and the harbours at its foot. The outer wall is twenty miles long and takes in the townlands to the West and whole of the lush northern suburb of Megara where the rich used to live. These days Megara is empty. The houses of the rich have been abandoned. The gardens grow wild.

The attack on Megara was unexpected. In the first year of the war there had been repeated attacks along the triple wall to the West and against the old citadel wall in the South. Those sections of the fortifications enclosing the northern suburbs had been untouched. The walls were manned night and day as a matter of course, but the garrisons were small. Roman patrols passed by out of range.

There was no warning, though they should have known. Aemilianus had come back, as commander-in-chief of the Roman forces. The stammering Mancinus was living in disgrace on his Campanian estate and by universal consent the young Mars was back. The men of the legions had come to believe that Carthage would only fall when the young hero took command. With his return the waiting war was ended.

One of the northern perimeter gates was forced by a Roman patrol in the early hours of the morning or opened by an act of treachery. No one knew. When the crisis was over and Hasdrubal had returned to the city with his troops he had some wretch hanged for the look of the thing, an old deaf janitor at one of the big houses near the wall. The old man went to his death shaking his head, ignorant of his crime. He was stone deaf and they could not make him understand.

It looked for a time as if the outer city would be lost. Roman troops were moving through the captured gate as day broke and there was no defence. By midday there were four thousand Roman infantrymen inside the wall, most of the Seventh Legion. With perfect Roman stolidity the invading troops halted inside the gate to throw up a makeshift bridgehead, ringing a few thousand square yards of gardens with hasty earthworks and felled date palms. These were providential hours for the defence of the city.

Defenders streamed out of the gates of the inner city, running down the tree-lined avenues toward Megara and the northern outer wall. It was a river of everyone who could be spared: reserve militia groups, women, slaves, the old, children.

The sun was westering before the first of the Roman maniples were forming up to move forward from their defences. The Carthaginians were waiting invisibly behind walls and hedges, in ditches and sunken lanes.

The Roman units advanced in their formations but the dressed lines began to break up as they moved into the labyrinth of walls and gardens. NCOs lost touch with other units, with their own men. The advance faltered almost immediately and panic-stricken fighting erupted in unseen and sudden ambushes and private episodes of frenzied slashing and stabbing among the hedges and ditches. In the semi darkness the Roman horns sounded the withdrawal and the invaders fell back behind their sketchy barriers.

The Carthaginians were out as soon as it was full night, women and men, crawling silently along ditch bottoms, squirming beneath felled trees, their naked bodies blackened with soot, filtering invisibly into the enemy's camp, cutting throats, spreading panic. Roman prisoners were brought out from the city jails and tortured through the night within earshot of their fellows.

And there was art in this. Tied to trees the wretched victims are cruelly goaded by Carthaginian widows with promises of intimate agonies to come. They cry out piteously to friends and comrades.

131

They sing songs and nursery rhymes in warbling falsettos as they watch the irons heating among the coals. The weird intolerable sounds carry through the hot night air. The cicadas are silent.

A mile away in the Roman camps on the isthmus the sound of screaming is faint, almost abstract, like the crying of night birds. Roman sentries inside the walls of Carthage are doubled, trebled and still they are mesmerised and undone and their piss runs out onto the ground. The armies of Rome fight in the daylight, in lines and columns. They are like boys and have no stomach for the secret horrors of the night. Aemilianus withdraws his troops in the evening of the third day after the incursion and the defenders reclaim the walls.

But the inhabitants of the suburb of Megara have gone. The rich, fearful and indignant, block the avenues with their carriages and litters as they struggle to gain the security of the inner city. There is panic and riot in suburbia. Carriages go over in the press as the tide of refugees flows toward the citadel gates. Children, the old, are crushed to death against the gates, trampled underfoot. The privileges of wealth are absolute.

Out on the plains Hasdrubal listens to the news of panic in the city with relief. Here is his excuse to re-enter the citadel. He is losing his war out here. It is a war which has been deprived of its logic. There are no longer Roman supply lines in Africa for his squadrons to attack. They bring in everything by sea through the port of Utica. Aemilianus is turning Africa into a wasteland. It is his strategy, simple, infallible, inhuman. If there is no food in all of Africa for the slimy Gugga vermin to buy, then they will starve. Hasdrubal knows in some part of himself that Carthage is already lost and that it would serve him better to cut and run now, to abandon his ragged army and take ship for Tyre, but he cannot resist the vision of his momentary triumph as he re-enters the city that condemned him. Little daydreams of private retribution fill his sleepless hours. He leaves Phameas the Numidian with a few cavalry squadrons outside the city to keep up the appearance of a war and re-enters the citadel at the head of his infantry columns.

His first public action after he has installed himself and his retinue in the Senate House on the Byrsa is to have all of the Roman prisoners brought out from their places of captivity in the city and tied to stakes at intervals along the rampart of the triple wall facing the Roman camps on the isthmus. There are some hundreds of these prisoners. They are mostly mules, legionaries, poor farmers driven to this war by poverty. There are some foreigners, Gauls and Dacians from legions raised in the provinces and a few young aristocrats, staff officers undone by the treachery of the time. They have paid handsomely for their commissions, their chance to be in at the kill, and here they are, blinking in the sun, starving, naked and verminous.

A few hundred yards away Romans are gathering along the palisaded rampart of their camp. Faces are recognised among the grimy scarecrows tied to their posts on the walls of the city. 'By God, it's Antoninus Pius. You remember, the thin fellow with a dose of the clap. We thought he'd crept home to mummy.' The fat man pulls a sword from its scabbard and begins to move down the line. The watchers mark the little lateral movement of Hasdrubal's sword across Antoninus Pius' belly and catch the small gush of dark entrails. He pauses before each naked wretch and hacks inexpertly, attempting to sever a foot, an arm, a head, genitals, but he is no swordsman. He grows breathless from the exertion and he pauses, panting, spattered crimson, looking out at the assembled thousands who have gathered along the Roman front to see. He motions his butchers forward and they advance along the line of posts chopping out the lives of the bound captives. The Romans watching from their ramparts are howling like wolves.

This is Hasdrubal's vengeance upon his native city. After this, no one will survive, no one.

And now the big houses in all the miles between the outer perimeter wall and the inner city are empty. The gardens of the rich have grown rank and riotous. A palm tree, toppled in the autumn gales, lies across the wide stone staircase that leads down to the baked brown lawns of Hasdrubal's house. Irrigation channels are choked and dry and the lush borders have been burnt brittle by the summer sun. Lizards bask in the dry fountains. In the once splendid atrium of his house the smell of fire and shit is strong. Obscenities in smeared excrement have dried black brown across the frescoes. Flies are loud in the spacious chambers. A terracotta bust lies in a shattered fan across the mosaic floor.

The whole exclusive suburb between the outer wall and the city wall is a no man's land. Deserters from the army of Rome and from the city lie up in wrecked mansions and summerhouses. Cut throats and derelicts and dog packs patrol the trampled paths. There are children out here too, cannibal troupes. A madman in a fantastical costume stands on a palace balcony as the sun sets. Close by him on the evening balustrade crouches his succubus: no ears, no nose, purulent and crooning, a quaint survival, a witness to the abominations committed upon his flesh by sooty demons. Once he was a soldier in the army of Rome. He is the madman's fool.

Megara is another country, a limbo between the starving city and the iron engines of Rome, death's hinterland, a dark border region abandoned of the spirit, the heart of darkness. Its denizens lie unmoving in derelict palaces through hot days. Sudden and outrageous deaths flower in burnt out rooms and abandoned gardens.

In the night Qart wades thigh deep a hundred yards out in the shallow sea for a mile past the Roman sentries on the beach. He can see soldiers silhouetted against the fires. Gusts of sparks drive down the black night wind. He has to swim where a buttress of the perimeter wall comes down into the sea. He can hear the water slapping distantly against the breakwater at the wall's foot. He is at home here, out in the black water, away from the fires and all comfort.

In the early dawn he swims in to the rocky shore and feels the water grow warmer as he comes in to the shallows. Scaling the red cindery slopes of the coast he comes down into the silent avenues of Megara in the half light of morning.

He is not unfamiliar with the outer city yet he finds it unintelligible. It has become a trackless place of burnt out buildings and blocked roads, a place he does not recognise. Road signs and street names have gone. He encounters corpses from last year's fighting heaped in dry ditches. He navigates by the risen sun glimpsed between dead palms, making by degrees for the distant wall of the inner city. The going is slow and he does not see a soul. He passes through a broken wall and traverses a wide parched lawn, punctuated by statuary. A stone seat is covered with blown palm debris. He clears a space and sits. Beyond the grass, black flags of soot stain the white marble walls of a mansion above burnt out windows. An ornate ormolu divan lies upside down on the steps outside the double doors and the doors themselves hang weirdly inward into darkness. He leans back against the seat and closes his eyes for a moment in the warmth of the sun and sleeps suddenly, going down like a stone into a well.

He wakes again, coming to himself out of the void. His eyes are closed and he listens behind his eyelids to the sounds. He can feel the light of morning on his eyelids as he concentrates. There is a movement to his left across the dry grass and another movement behind him. Through the lattice of his eyelashes he watches the patch of burnt grass before him and sets the whole of his being to the space at his back. A shadow waits at the edge of his field of vision, then begins to advance noiselessly toward him. The arms of the shadow begin to go up and the shape of a stick or a sword detaches itself.

Qart is up and the knife is already in his hand. The razor point goes in low, hardly above the pelvic bone and he lifts it upward through the lumpy masses of the gut letting out a cascade of livid blue and yellow onto the thirsty ground. The blade hits the breastbone and he clutches his enemy to him, holding him up. They are like lovers. The creased unshaven cheek lies next to his own and he feels the hot fluttering spasms of breath. He feels the wet heat of opened guts against his body. They turn like dancers together to receive the jolt of the axe blade. Qart smiles at the axeman. He drops his lover and the buried axe is carried downward. His knife comes free, effortless, post coital, and flickers outward, hardly to be seen. The criss cross benediction of the blade opens the arteries at either side of the axeman's neck. He is a fountain. Crimson gush boils out of him. He runs about like an actor, his hands gripped to the sides of his neck, sending scarlet arabesques across the parched grass as he spins and staggers. He falls and gets up again, falls again and does not get up, though the strange sounds he is making go on for some time. Someone else is running away. Qart turns to see a movement through the far hedge, a disappearance. He looks down at his clothes, at the mess he has made.

37

The scribe has the afternoon watch. He volunteers as usual for the water detail along the citadel wall. It means carrying the heavy waterskins and he has to rest often but he prefers it. He has grown used to it. Walking round the wall tops of the inner city takes up the whole watch. He stops at the sentry posts and doles out the water ration to the men, using the regulation iron cup as a measure. He exchanges a little gossip.

He sets off from the public wells near the Tophet, he and the once fat barber who used to work across the street from where he lives, carrying the water skins. Kolomon is the barber's name. For years Spendios knew his face but not his name. Now he knows his name. He had the shop next to the Italian cobbler who was hanged.

At the wells by the Tophet, soldiers lounge in the shade and the water has to be signed for. Hasdrubal has posted troops at all of the public wells to supervise the rationing of water. The women who come down each day for water must run the leering gauntlet.

Spendios and Kolomon the barber, who used to be fat, walk along the side of the outer harbour with the dripping waterskins and cross the lock bridge to that part of the wall which overlooks the sea. They climb up the stone steps to the wall top and come out above the blue blank stare of the sea. They gaze out for a moment together.

Sometimes Spendios thinks of the day he watched the little hostages being taken on to the Roman ships just a hundred yards away from where he stands now and sometimes he thinks of how the deserted sea-front used to be, in the old days, before the war.

The barber sometimes thinks of the same things. Sometimes they speak about what they are thinking but mostly they just think, often the same things, sometimes at the same time. Occasionally the barber wonders what the thin girl at the city bakery looks like without her dress. The barber moves off to the right along the ruined wall top toward the harbour mouth. When he gets above the Choma, the wide rectangular quay which lies to the seaward side of the wall, he will lower his water skins on a rope to the men of the garrison there. He will return with the empty skins to the Tophet wells and return again to the Choma with two more full ones. In the time it takes him to do these tasks the scribe will have traversed the whole of the rest of the wall gradually doling out his own water to the men of the sentry posts.

It takes Spendios ten minutes to walk that stretch of the wall which runs north along the sea front to the place where the city wall abuts it. He measures out water for the two sentries posted there and turns inland along the top of the old city wall. Below him to the left are the backs of tenements. To his right, outside the wall, a vista of dead palm tops and umbrella pines stretches away as far as he can see, with a glimpse here and there of an overgrown garden gate or the tiled roof of a house. Nothing moves outside the wall. Nobody lives in Megara now, not since the fighting last year and the entry of Hasdrubal's army into the citadel

The wall top is stepped up for a few yards above each gate. There are three gates in this stretch of the wall and he has fallen into the habit of resting for a while above the middle one. A palm-lined avenue recedes northward to the suburbs from below his feet as he stands over the gate. As a child he used to walk along the wall top just as he is walking now and stand up here above the gate to watch the carriages of the rich passing in and out below him and the gaudy litters. Walking around the walls was something that people did in those days, for pleasure. There were no soldiers on the battlements in those days.

The gate is barred now and nothing moves along the avenue. The road surface is littered with brash and palm debris and fans of wind-blown sand. A hundred yards out a carriage lies on its side, untouched since the flight of the rich into the city. Beyond the ruined carriage the deserted roadway and the straight rows of tall palms draw distantly together. A mote moves in his eye. Nothing. Something again, something like memory, a tiny movement in and out of shadow. He waits. Finally it is a movement, a figure, someone walking out of the abandoned wilderness. Tiny at first, hardly there

137

at all, half a mile out on the long straight avenue, the figure approaches by little and little. It is a man, walking unhurriedly as if he were out for a stroll. He carries no bag, no luggage, a thin man with pale hair. He is walking down the middle of the road and at last with perfect inevitability he comes beneath the gate where the scribe is. The man stops and looks up.

As a citizen soldier of the Thitmanit District Militia, Spendios is supposed to carry a spear at all times when he is on duty. He can't remember when he last saw his spear. It might be standing among the hung up coats at home. His mother objected to him leaving it by the door. 'What are we, cut-throats, footpads?' He wishes he had it now. He looks back the way he has come along the parapet and he cannot see the sentries, but then his eyes are not what they were. He wishes he had his spear. He feels exposed without his spear. If he had a spear he would know what to do. The man is still standing in the middle of the road looking up at him. Spendios calls out, as if he were behind his own front door in his dressing gown, not defending a whole city from invaders.He has no idea what he is going to do. He feels ridiculous, though he has no choice but to do something. What he really wants to do is crouch down out of sight until the strange man goes away. He shouts down,

'Yes?'

The man continues to look up at him and the scribe feels a certain irritation. This is not how it should be. Spendios tries again with an attempt at a peremptory tone.

'Speak. What have you got to say?'

There is a pause during which Spendios wonders if the stranger understands Punic. Perhaps he is a foreigner. He is about to address him in Latin though he does not look like an Italian, when the man speaks. His voice is low, polite.

'What would you like me to say?'

'How should I know?'

This creates a sort of impasse. At last the stranger says in his reasonable voice,

'Suppose I said that I have an important message for Hasdrubal.'

'Then I suppose I should let you in.'

There is a stone stair which descends at the back of the gateway from the parapet to the ground. Spendios goes down and stands there in the shade of the arch behind the massive gates. He looks for a place where he might squint through, but the gates are solid. He is not at all sure that he is doing the right thing. There are two bars resting in iron brackets across the gates, which slide into long recesses in the stonework. He manages to slide the lower bar away but then he has to pull it out again so that he can stand on it to move the upper bar. He reaches up and the dust of months falls into his eyes. The bar is very heavy and he can only move it a little at a time. He is breathless and giddy with exertion by the time he has managed to slide both bars into the wall. He pulls the heavy door open a fraction. The man has been pushing from the outside and his face is suddenly a foot from his own. Spendios jumps. The man smiles at him, a faint glacial smile. Together they move the door enough for the stranger to pass inside. He helps Spendios to push it shut and to reposition the heavy bars. They brush down their clothes with their hands. The stranger's garment is stained rust red down the front.

'Do you have an important message for Hasdrubal?'

'No.'

'No? Then what are you doing here? This is no place to be. There is nothing to eat.'

'One has to be somewhere.'

Spendios ponders this.

'Of course you'll have to come with me to the guardhouse. You'll have to talk to the commander. This isn't my responsibility you know.'

'Of course.'

'Well, come along then.'

Spendios struggles to lift the straps of the heavy waterskins over his shoulders. The stranger takes them from him and puts them across his own shoulders. Spendios looks doubtful for a moment, unsure if this is some breach of military protocol. He shrugs.

'You'll just have to follow me. I have my rounds to do, you see. Come along.'

The scribe ascends the stone stairs to the wall top and the stranger follows. The two figures recede along the ancient parapet. Spendios' voice sounds clearly out of the distance.

'We're late. Come along.'

Arrad, the commander of the Thitmanit District Militia, is a moneylender. Money lending has been good to him. He was never poor and recently he has grown rich. These last years he has grown very rich by accepting fashionable houses and properties in the city as security on loans he has arranged for people fleeing the city. He has split up these houses into rooms and makes money as a landlord. The rich left the city in fear. The poor arrived from their outlying villages in fear, seeking the security of the city and its walls. He likes being a landlord and thinks that he should have gone into the property business years ago. He likes the deference he gets from the tenants, likes it even better when the rent is in arrears and he can fondle the unprotesting wives and mothers when he visits unexpectedly in the middle of the day. He likes to visit his tenants in the middle of the day, when the husbands are absent.

'Doomed city, pish,' he says to his wife at the dinner table. 'Business is good. Business is very good.'

He had always intended to leave the city when the time came. A few ships still came and went despite the blockade. He would get away, when the time came. He has his investments abroad, in Delos, Rhodes, has planned ways and means, but somehow the time never quite came. Business was always just a little too brisk, a little too full of promise.

And then, as in a bad dream it is too late.

Fat Hasdrubal has returned to the city with his army and issued a series of edicts, a list of treasonable crimes. They are posted around the city everywhere, inescapably, in several languages. Edict number five states that anyone found attempting to leave Carthage is to be executed without trial. Whole families are dragged from the holds of merchant ships and hanged at the harbour entrance, people the moneylender knows, business associates – like a bad dream. Arrad sends one of his clerks down to the harbour with money, bullion, to sound out the military stationed at the harbour. Neither the slave nor the money return. There is a rumour that captured fugitives are being disembowelled by Hasdrubal's troops in search of the gold coins they are supposed to have swallowed.

His money buys him some things. He does not starve like the mob and can send his slaves out to buy food on the black market, though the prices are criminal, but his money will not save him from the Romans. He bought the command of the Thitmanit District Militia and it saves him the exertions of guard duty and gives him a certain immunity, but his money will not save him from the Romans.

This revelation haunts him through his waking hours and on the helpless treadmills of his dreams. It seems impossible. His bladder flutters and one day soon, when the vision invades him he will wet himself. He keeps money under the floor, gold coins. Each week he adds another bag as if he were putting offerings on an altar, which of course is what he is doing. When they break down the door he will hold out his money. He will kneel in supplication, holding out his money. He will be a holy beggar offering money. His money will save him. How can it not? He rehearses the moment endlessly in his head as he sits at his desk with his legs crossed so that he does not wet himself.

He cannot make his wife understand. She goes about her domestic business as always and she does it all so brightly now, so gaily, though she no longer goes out of the house. She has had the shutters on the windows overlooking the street nailed shut. When he tries to speak of what is to come it is as if she cannot hear his voice. She tells him that she is planning a party. She is making a guest list. When he rages at her she talks through his noise about the flower arrangements and about who will sit next to whom. When he falls to silent weeping she tells him in her bright quavery voice about the menu, the place settings. She shows him the invitations she has written, to couples long since fled, to the couple whose shrunken corpses still sway by the harbour.

When Spendios brings the stranger to his desk Arrad is rehearsing his speech to the soldiers who have broken down his door. He is sitting on the chair in his empty office with his eyes closed and his legs crossed, intoning the words of supplication.

Qart becomes a member of the scribe's unit. He is issued with the ration tokens which will allow him to starve more slowly and his name is added to the rotas. He takes his watches on the ramparts and spends days with the dead carts. Deaths in the city have become too numerous for the civil authorities and the militia groups are allotted days for collecting and burying the corpses in the pits

141

which have been dug to the north of the Byrsa. The old mostly, and the very young, sapped and stretched for too long on starvation's rack, they fly up grey and weightless on to the piled carts. In the narrow streets the white lime hangs in a cloud about the cart and the mortuary men are as white as corpses themselves.

The spy lodges with the scribe in his tenement flat. The autumn weather is mild and he sleeps on the flat roof among the dead pot plants and the washing lines. Spendios' mother takes immediately to the stranger and his old fashioned good manners. The old woman has grown transparent in these years of want. Her fierce spirit burns in its too fragile censer of lucent bone. The daylight seems almost to shine through her as she sits with her lacework outside on the balcony. Qart sits by her, winding her lace bobbins, listening to her tales.

He is no trouble. He sweeps the stairs of the tenement each week. He has planted squashes and cucumbers in old buckets on the rooftop. In the evenings he goes up to the roof with books he borrows from Spendios and reads with a blanket around him until the light has gone. He cooks his meagre rations up there too, over a little earthenware bowl of charcoal. Occasionally he will sit with Spendios and his mother playing cards, skat, piquet.

Spendios comes up the ladder to the roof. The sun has gone down and the sky is a mysterious lilac. The jumbled rooftops stepping down the hill toward the harbours are empty of people. Before the war they would have been out in their deck chairs drinking wine. Evenings on the roof gardens were convivial, sociable. You might have heard a song or a melody drifting up from the street or a burst of laughter in the twilight. In those days the rooftops were gardens with vine arbours and palm trees growing from broken amphorae and the smell of wisteria in the darkness. These days the rooftops are empty. There is no wine to drink in the evenings, no reason to sing, no cause for laughter.

They have been on the dead carts all day, he and the stranger, and Spendios can see him now, his head still white with lime dust, squatting by his bowl of charcoal among his buckets of seedlings, cooking. Spendios can smell the food. The savour is rich, sweetish, troubling. It is not the smell of millet porage. He moves across to where the stranger is turning a strip of meat in the little wavering column of heat. The meat spits and pops a little and the scribe's mouth is full of saliva. He can barely remember the last meat he ate. There is no meat in Carthage. Even the dogs have been eaten. He says out of his thought,

'Meat?'

The stranger cuts a piece from the strip and holds it out to Spendios between his thumb and his knife.

'Wolf.'

Spendios does not take the proffered mouthful. He says,

'There are no wolves in Carthage.'

The stranger shrugs and pops the pale scorched fragment into his own mouth.

38

Picture this. Fat Hasdrubal is standing on a little podium made of wood, fantastical in the frogged splendour of his dress uniform, haranguing a group of bemused Roman staff officers. A tasseled rope barrier has been set about the podium as if to keep back the press of his audience. It is not clear to the Romans what the fat man is doing here or why he has arranged this meeting out beyond the triple wall of the city. Aemilianus sits his horse among his general staff listening to the translator with a kind of suspended disbelief.

Hasdrubal has grown fatter, become gross beyond all decency. In the famished city of Carthage he is the gluttonous other, starvation's bloated angel. He gorges nightly on the dreams of the city's starving thousands. He eats until he is sick then eats again, ravished by disgust.

He is reading a prepared address. He is reasoning with his audience, laying out his case. It is like a play. There are thespian flourishes and arch asides. At Aemilianus' stirrup the interpreter's expression betrays his intense and troubled concentration as he struggles to render the rhetorical figures into a prosaic Latin. It is not clear to the Romans what this obese clotheshorse is about. They catch one another's eyes quizzically. He seems to be petitioning for terms, not for the city but for himself. Can this hippopotamus really be asking for large sums of money to quit the city, for safe conduct for himself and his extensive household? Can it really be a private arrangement he is seeking? What about his civic duty, his responsibility to the starving thousands behind the walls? Aemilianus leans down from his horse and says to the translator,

'Tell him No.'

The factotum calls across the space. A shadow passes momentarily across Hasdrubal's face. He loses his place in the prepared text.

'Tell him he is a disgrace to his city. Tell him we have not forgotten the public butchery of Roman prisoners.'

The interpreter calls across to the podium again. A little enactment of comic disbelief plays across the fat orator's face as he fixes the wretched factotum with his gaze. Hasdrubal shuffles his sheets of paper until he finds the one he is searching for, his alternative text. He holds the new sheet before him and begins again, differently this time, declaiming in patriotic tones. The translator does what he can.

Polybius the Greek, in a surviving fragment of his history of the war, renders a part of the fat man's speech as follows,

'I call upon the Gods and upon Fortune to witness my oath. I swear that the day will never come when I, Hasdrubal son of Giscon, will gaze at the same time upon the sun in the sky and upon my own unhappy city consumed by fire. The most noble funeral for a right minded man is to perish in his native city and amid her flames.'

Hasdrubal lifts his head and gazes at Aemilanus for a long moment before he turns and steps down from his platform. He sways slowly and with vast composure back across the parched and unkempt space toward the gate in the city wall. His retainers pull up the rope barrier and pile it hurriedly on the makeshift podium. They scurry after Hasdrubal, carrying it like a litter. Aemilianus' men glance at one another, nonplussed.

39

The darkness is a wind that has neither form nor limit. There is nothing but the wind. Hanno is leaning against the steering oar with his sodden cloak beating invisibly at his knees. He is cold. It seems to him as if he has always been cold. He sees nothing, only the blotched and leaping black.

He feels the bow lift as the ship begins its slow climb up the swell, the next long ramp of ocean. He sees nothing. At the mountain summit, at the wimpling wave crest, the wind redoubles, driving unseen spray like hail. He is out of time, alive only to the raging wind's buffet and the mountain ranges of the sea.

Out where the horizon should be he glimpses a thread separating itself along the black, hardly there, before the ship begins its long descent into the abyss. At the next howling wave crest Hanno sees that the horizontal thread has become a faintly fuming pallor, dividing the darkness from the darkness. It is the dark dawn, the transfixing first light of day. Hanno is born again to the seen, to the dun lift of ocean.

In the level light of sunrise the *Osiris* passes through the pillars of Melquart, re-entering the world, leaving the long grey swells of the Western Ocean astern. She is back, her paintwork faded to bleached wood, the bellying sail patched and stained and ragged. Three years gone, lost to the world among the Northern Isles and the *Osiris* is wallowing home at last under her cargo of blue tin and black jet.

Hanno is standing by the steersman, squinting into the unfamiliar blue dazzle. His hair is long, stiff and matted with salt spray and a patterned blue tattoo runs across his forehead and down the bridge of his nose. The crew are the same, worse: blue painted pigtailed savages. They are returning from the world's edge, from the isles of oblivion.

The ship sails westward for a day along the coast of Iberia with the smell of thyme coming off the land like memory. They are a week from home, a week from Carthage. They are men reborn. The ship puts in at the port of Malaka in the sleepy sunlit afternoon. The blueness of the water in the harbour is strange and the scintillation of the sunlight across its surface makes Mattho the mate dewy eyed. He weeps for reasons he cannot name.

In the town they are stared at and pointed at as they wander about the market with their pockets full of Pictish gold, aching for what is familiar. Moustachioed whores call down from balconies and the crew pause beneath, looking up their skirts. Even a brothel seems strange to them after so long. They troop up awkwardly.

Hanno is sitting outside a bar at the edge of the market place. The stallholders are beginning to pack up for the day. Mattho comes out with the drinks. He says with no trace of a smile,

'Red wine. They don't have beer.'

They drink in silence, watching the market place empty. Boys are dismantling stalls, sweeping the day's rubbish into piles. There is a slight movement of unfamiliar warmth in the air, a half forgotten softness. At the far side of the market place the sea is a strip of turquoise and the masts of the moored ships move against the glitter, confusing the eye. There is luxury in the softness of the air, in the lilac light, in the first opulent hit of the wine.

Mattho is reaching forward in his mind to the city of Carthage, to the house where he lives near the city wall, to his family and the children who will not know him. He sees his wife with her round belly as in a miniature painting, shouting after him as he runs from his house down to the dock to catch the *Osiris* before she clears the outer harbour. Voicing his thoughts he says,

'It's a girl. I had a dream. She'll be walking by now. Talking. She takes after her mother. In my dream.'

Hanno raises his glass benevolently.

'To Kankanaya's little sister.'

A barman is collecting glasses. He makes routine conversation with the foreign sailors.

'Carthage? You don't look like Carthaginians. Where you going now then?'

'Home.'

'To Carthage?'

'That's right.'

The barman's movements as he wipes the table slow to a stop.

'You been away long, have you?'

146

'Three years.'

'Don't you know then?'

'Know what?'

'You don't know, do you? Here Julio...'

He calls to the barman inside.

'...there's two Carthaginian blokes here, just back from foreign parts and they don't know.'

Julio comes out wiping his hands on a towel to see these prodigies. There is a moment in which nothing is said, in which the barmen struggle apprehensively for the right thing to say.

'Three years you been away?'

'That's right. Three years, and a bit.'

'There's a war, see. It's the Romans....'

'A what?'

'It's the Romans. You can't get into Carthage.'

'No end of businesses here, you know, here in Malaka have gone bust... shippers, traders, all sorts. Carthage used to be a magnet, a great big magnet. Everything went through Carthage. But since the war nothing goes in or comes out. You wouldn't believe. Business is bad everywhere. The whole coast. Even this bar...'

'I heard tell that they're going to pull it down brick by brick, once they get inside. Kill everybody. It doesn't do to mess with the Romans.'

'They got an army. They got warships. They sink anything that goes near.'

'I lost my brother in law last year. Trying to run the blockade he was, with a load of olive oil. Them blockade ships are fast. He was rammed from both sides. Ship sank, just like that. The Romans shot 'em all to death in the water. My sister hasn't been the same since she heard.'

'I don't know what them Carthaginians have been eating these last two years.'

Darkness has fallen. The moon is rising hugely above the empty market place and the expanses of paving stones shine pearly white. The black shape of a dog moves about sniffing the silvery ground.

Hanno and Mattho are still sitting outside the bar. They have been drinking. They are drunk. Hanno says for the twentieth time.

'Don't worry. We'll get there. We'll sail in... through the blockade.'

Mattho's silence is eloquent. Hanno puts his hand on the mate's forearm.

'No, listen. We come in late in the day after sunset when the wind is onshore and there's less chance of being spotted. Moonlight. We'll do it when the moon is full. They'll never even see us. With the wind astern the blockade ships won't even sniff us. We can hit the harbour in one, clean as a whistle. That channel will take two Tyrian galleys side by side. I could steer that channel blindfold.'

Mattho shakes off his hand and reaches for the bottle. He is sullen drunk and will not be appeased. Hanno blathers into the dangerous silence.

'I know. I know. I've kept you away again.'

'Three fucking years, that's all. You've stolen my life you bastard. And now my wife and kids are shut up inside Carthage with nothing to eat.'

'Look, I'm sorry. I'm sorry.'

'Sorry? You bastard.'

The table goes over. The two men are on the ground, struggling. Mattho has his hands in Hanno's hair and he is banging his head against the underside of the fallen table and weeping like a baby.

40

Scipio's causeway creeps yard by yard toward the choma across the deepwater channel at the mouth of the harbour. The long lines of ox carts laden with stone move up and back without cease, day and night. The loads of white stone slide into the indigo sea with a noise that can be heard from the city walls.

At the beginning, when the carts began dumping stone into the sea at the far side of the channel the Carthaginians were contemptuous. A hundred and fifty yards of water divides the beach from the harbour wall. The channel is too deep, too wide. Big Tyrian galleys used to pass each other abreast entering and leaving the harbour. The mathematicians argue about how many millions of tons of stone the task would require, how many thousands of man-hours. It would take them ten years, twenty.

In six weeks the causeway is more than half complete and the mathematicians have stopped arguing. With each yard gained the wooden siege towers which have stood these many months on the beach waiting for the time, are edged out along its roadway. From the topmost platforms of these towers, which stand twenty feet higher than the city wall the Roman catapult crews dominate the walls on either side of the harbour mouth. The defenders on the city walls stay out of sight, unable to fire down upon the slow queues of carts. A helmet raised above the parapet on a stick survives for a few moments in the skipping and sparking storm of bolts from the belly shooters on the towers, before it spins away crushed and deformed. At night Roman onagers lob phosphorous flares high over the harbour so that any movement on the city walls can be seen in the green white dazzle. The work proceeds without interruption and the causeway grows inexorably closer to that part of the city wall which defends the choma.

It is an hour before daybreak, the cold dark before the dawn. Qart stands in the shadow of the battlement in this dead of night watching the crawling thousands out on the causeway. It is an army of the night, countless points of torchlight in the darkness. A universe of answering reflections dance in the unseen breathing sea. A flare lifts away from the platform of a siege tower, its leprous white light blooming at the black zenith, and the dreadful ant army is revealed in the falling sulphurous dazzle. And when the black engulfs the guttering debris again as it falls to earth, afterimages loop and convulse. There is a blind moment before the points of torchlight register again upon his eye.

He watches again. Soon the night shift will change. There will be a pause, a hardly-to-be-seen forming up of men. Columns will march back along the causeway. There will be a brief time, a space of a few minutes when the whole length of the mole will be still and the fixed torches will burn silently in their brackets and then the new shift will arrive, the new columns, and the work will begin again.

'Suicide.'

'Possibly.'

'Swim, you say?'

'We get into the water in the harbour and wait out of sight close to the sea wall until the watch begins to change on the mole. We swim the hundred yards to the causeway and set fire to the towers in the time it takes for the morning watch to march up from the beach.'

'Anything else?'

'We carry flint and tinder around our necks in leather pouches. We pull floating sacks of oil soaked rag. The iron chain at the harbour entrance will need to be lowered so that we can swim through.'

'Anything else?'

The tone is only mildly sarcastic. Qart appears not to notice. He continues in his reasonable voice.

'We go naked...'

A raised eyebrow. The adjutant can't quite get the measure of what is being said to him.

'...and we paint our bodies, like devils.'

The adjutant watches Qart. The sarcasm grows ponderous to the point of foolishness.

'Like devils? What a good idea.'

'The Romans are afraid of the dark. They are credulous, superstitious.'

The adjutant is struggling. He does not know what to make of this thin man. He is ruffled and confused by the new man's intense and absolute composure; so he blusters, naturally.

'Your suggestion is preposterous. You want my permission to recruit volunteers for this escapade?'

Qart turns his gaze upon the adjutant and says in his reasonable voice,

'The Romans will kill us all, whatever happens. They will destroy the whole city. We are dead men. Nothing matters. They are irresistible and we resist them. There is nothing else.'

The adjutant does not know if this is treasonable defeatism he is listening to or the voice of madness. Hasdrubal has made it a capital offence to speak of defeat. The adjutant's mouth opens and shuts like a fish.

41

The *Osiris* raises her anchors and leaves the roadstead of Lilybaeum in the dark before the dawn, passing between the black hulls of Roman transports and out through quiet constellations of lamp-lit fishing boats that lie spread across the sea's back.

When the sun comes up on the port side they are out of sight of the land. There are only three men on board, Hanno, Mattho and Aris the Berber. The rest of the crew are in the bars and brothels of Lilybaeum, paid off, rich for the moment. They know that they are locked out of Carthage, stranded like men on the moon but Hanno has told them that he is taking the ship to Carthage anyway. He gives them the choice, pay off in Sicily or try their luck against the ships of Rome. All of them except black Aris have chosen the fleshpots of Lilybaeum. Hanno has sold the cargo of tin to the armourers' guild in Lilybaeum town. The guild have their offices near the civic baths. He has left the crates of jet in a warehouse.

Aris has no ties in Carthage, no family. He is a private man not given to unnecessary speech and Hanno does not enquire. The ship is just about manageable in fair weather with three. Without Aris they would be in trouble. Hanno knows that they will be in trouble anyway. He is not drunk now.

They raise Cape Terror on the African coast about noon and the fortress on its headland is in ruins. A new wooden watchtower has been built on the cliff top. Hanno steers a course out into the Gulf of Carthage away from the coast, away from the watchtower.

The faint ghost of the horned mountain hangs on the horizon through the afternoon and at last they catch the dim white smudge that is Carthage. Mattho's eyes are good and he sees something that might be a galley, a warship, and so they lower the sail and wait for the night and the freshening of the onshore wind. Under bare poles the *Osiris* is still making a little way in the breeze. They throw out the sea anchor and wait.

Mattho stands in the bow with his eyes on the dun filament that is the coast hearing the idle slap of wavelets against the hull. A mass of waterlogged timber floating level with the surface, masts and spars tangled together with cordage, a relic of some wreck, moves slowly by at a distance. He walks back to where Hanno and Aris are squatting against the bulwark. Aris is cracking almond shells with a marlinspike and eating the nuts. He keeps the broken shells swept together on the deck by his leg in a tidy pile. He passes every other one to Hanno. The mate says,

'What about the chain?'

'What chain?'

'The chain. The fucking iron chain with links as fat as your arm that they winch up across the harbour mouth. That fucking chain.'

'Oh, that chain.'

A pause. Aris offers Mattho a shelled almond.

'Well?'

'Well, what?'

'What's going to happen?'

'How do I know?'

'We hit that chain at speed and we're fucked.'

'Look, I'm not a magician. We go in close to the harbour wall. If the chain's up and we hit it then we might be able to get up onto the dock side, you know, not drown, like that, maybe.'

'I can't swim.'

'Neither can I.'

'You'll damage the ship.'

'I think that there's a good chance the Romans will damage the ship before we ever get to the sodding chain. Put a big ram hole in it below the water line. That kind of thing. You know, shoot us to death in the water.'

The mate walks across the deck and looks out at the floating spars. He says, without turning round,

'You don't have to do this.'

'Yes I do.'

Mattho glances at the drifting spars again and then he goes back to the bow to watch the coast.

The sun goes down, sinking behind the distant city into mauve obscurity. The evening wind rises and the cordage rattles against the mast. Hanno has come up behind the mate where he stands by the stem post and they wait together on the lonely sea, watching for the same thing. The light thickens toward darkness. Hanno says,

'We should have known.'

'But they always light the beacons at dusk. Always.'

'Not when there's a war on, they don't. We should have thought. We should have known.'

'You can't do it in the dark without the beacons.'

'I told you, I can do it blindfold. Watch me.'

On his way back to the after deck he stops at the mast and flicks the mainsail sheet free of its cleat. The big sail drops with a clatter and fills with the night wind.

42

There are twenty of them. They have tied up their hair and pushed their knives through the topknots to be out of the way. Around their necks they wear amulets, pouches containing flint and tinder. They listen to the slow clanking of the windlass pawls in the darkness as the iron chain at the harbour mouth is lowered. Their thin painted bodies are tiger striped, black and yellow and they go one by one down the vertical ladder into the sepulchral waters of the harbour like devils going down into Hell. They tread the black water holding on to the floating fuel sacks.

Qart swims toward the harbour mouth, keeping to the deep moon shadow of the dock wall and they follow him with hardly a splash, hardly a glint of folded water in the moonlight.

He comes out between the pillars of the harbour entrance into the silver light of open water. There is a wind out here and rags of cloud scud across the moon. A hundred yards off, the three siege towers loom against the moonlit sky, black behemoths. A flare lifts into the sky turning night to spectral day. Qart waits, treading water as the green-white dazzle droops and diminishes to darkness again. To his right, torches are moving away along the causeway as the night shift centuries depart.

They make the crossing of the swinging wind furrowed swell

unseen, swimming through spinning cats' paws. Qart's bare feet find the steep stony bank of the causeway and he waits shivering, half in and half out of the water until they have all reached the shallows at either side of him. From where they are they can see nothing of the causeway roadbed a few feet above. Only the tops of the towers are to be seen huge and black against the flying cloud. He moves up the steep stones and they follow, dragging the sacks. Stones clatter noisily into the water.

Qart comes out crouching into the open. Nothing. The men begin to emerge behind him. He waves them across to the first tower and as they go stooping and running with the sacks into the moon shadow of the tower, he sees the Romans.

Three, four of them maybe, in a tight group, moving uncertainly away from the second tower, watchmen. Their heads move this way and that as they crane into the darkness. Qart begins to run toward them, hallooing and capering fantastically. When he is a few yards away and he is sure that they have seen him he crouches on his hams and waves his arms above his head and crows. He rolls and clowns closer, mesmerising them with his antics. There are four of them. Two of them carry spears. They are laughing and making jokes, free of apprehension now, embarrassed by their own nervousness. Just some painted lunatic. Qart tumbles tipple tail toward them and as he goes over he pulls the knife from the topknot of his hair. He arrives among their feet in a heap. They are laughing boisterously and poking him with the ends of their spears. There is a moment in which he composes himself for what is about to happen and then he rises up with a corkscrew motion, the knife in his outstretched hand, opening great sliced wounds as he spins upward. They reel away gushing and whimpering and he pursues them. He kills two and loses two among the shadows.

As he kneels over his second man, over the last loosening shudder, he is aware of long wind blown flames uncoiling from the tower to his left. Among the racing skeins of sparks the others are running toward him, toward the second tower, with their torches.

To his right the men of the fourth legion are marching up along the causeway, thousands of them, the morning shift men. He can almost sense the moment when the two bleeding fugitives arrive among the approaching Romans. He can hear shouting, shouted orders. Somewhere beyond the third tower they are beginning to deploy into lines.

Close by, the second tower is aflame. Smoky veils of red are snaking upward. Fifty yards further off the first tower is a roaring column of fire a hundred feet high and the heat is palpable. The naked men are rapt in their work and are starting to run along the causeway again toward the third tower with their torches. Romans are appearing, spreading like a dark tide around its base.

Qart is running again, fantastical and demonic, out of the smoke and the flames. The painted man is running screaming at his enemies. The other devils are running too, caught up in his madness. To the Roman troops in the front lines they are a vision from a nightmare and the whole formation wavers and recoils. Qart has reached the line, slashing and capering and crying out and they are dissolving away from him, away from the flickering razor arcs of his knife. They cringe and cower away from his wanton and abhorrent folly and he opens them up as he pleases. It is a visitation, an hallucination of naked demons. The whole mass of troops is convulsing as terror takes its hold upon them, and then they are running away, fighting their way back through their comrades, clawing and bereft of sense.

With a torch in his hand Qart is climbing the last dark tower from one ladder to the next. He is looking for the onager. He knows from his nights on the ramparts of the city that it is from top of this great engine that the nightlong flares rise into the darkness. He comes up gasping through the final floor and emerges into the open, bloodied and grinning like a stage devil. The crew are cowering behind the catapult. The naked man merely ignores them and as he walks about the platform they dodge away round eyed, keeping the catapult between him and them. The incendiaries are piled by the catapult under damp sacking, fused parcels wrapped in string and coated with wax, big as a human head and about as heavy. He lights two of the fuses with his torch where they lay and steps back down the ladder.

He is two ladder lengths down when the night above him begins to turn to day. White light and midnight shadows leap among the heavy timbers as he flees. It is blinding noon in the baulked and laddered mineshaft of the tower's interior. In a series of overlapping detonations the top of the tower explodes in fulminating brilliance, a new sun blossoming in the darkness. A hundred miles away down the coast they watch the glow in the sky and think that Carthage has fallen and that the city is burning.

The naked men are running back to the end of the causeway. Resurrected, born again, they take to the dark water like new souls, avid for survival.

At the base of the mole, where it joins the beach Romans are killing Romans. Scipio Aemilianus has sent cavalry units to stop the rout and to drive the terror stricken troops back to confront the enemy. In the darkness the fighting is desperate and formless.

Under full sail the *Osiris* comes tearing out of the black night into the lurid glare. She plunges through the wave crests in bursting clouds of spray. She is picked out against the black in the rising shimmer of the fires, a spectral ghost ship. For the watchers on the walls of Carthage it is another prodigy in a night of prodigies.

Hanno and Mattho and Aris are leaning together with the weight of their bodies against the steering oar and the ship comes hard over, heeling perilously, turning for the harbour mouth. They cannot believe what they see. Three gigantic towers of flame are roaring into the sky where the harbour entrance should be. Mattho is shouting and crying.

'Oh fuck, oh fuck, oh fuck, where's the fucking dock gate? They built a fucking wall! Don't mess with the Romans. Don't mess with the fucking Romans. I told you. I told you.'

The *Osiris* is piling toward destruction through the livid sea, a vision of impending catastrophe in the white green dazzle. Aris grabs Hanno by the shoulder and points. The mole is not complete. The harbour entrance has not yet been sealed. To the right! To the right, is that a channel, a narrow channel between the end of the stone barrier and the wall of the choma?

Hanno has seen it and has already in that simple epiphany of seeing become the engine of the act. In that same and indistinguishable moment he hauls the ship hard round beneath the towering infernos under a rain of burning debris, shaving the causeway with a great grinding of stones against the hull. For a

156

moment the ship staggers into the wind away from the mole. He can see painted devils running along its crest. It is all of a lunatic piece. He waits, balancing impossibilities, watching the piled stones pass him one by one, slower and slower as in an inescapable dream. The last possible moment is closing like a door and the ship seems to hang motionless. He begins to ease her into the darkness that may be a navigable channel. She comes round in the same dream of fatal lassitude, slower and slower, with the contrary gusts chattering in the rigging. Stones grumble beneath the keel. He glimpses lines of troops advancing past the columns of fire.

A sudden black gust bats the sail and the yard swings violently across as the ship jibes. The rattling sail claps full of urgent wind and the vessel grinds on and over. Clear water under the keel. The *Osiris* passes between the stone columns of the sea gate, the last ship in all the world to enter the city of Carthage.

Hanno stands blankly as the ship loses way entirely in the lee of the silent lock. The *Osiris* drifts in the sudden quiet of the dark, empty harbour. Mattho is at his ear, demanding incredulously,

'What happened to the chain? What happened to the fucking chain?'

'Chain? What chain?'

A painted devil is swimming in the water below.

43

There is something fatal in this burning of the siege towers, as if their destruction were an act of magic, a ritual key turned in the lock to the door through which the destruction of the city itself will pass.

The smoking ruins stand on the empty causeway in a false and profound silence through the morning that follows the raid. The watchers on the walls mark the arrival of Roman burial parties. There is a little activity here and there, and then the long embankment is empty again. Imminence gathers through the hours. The three destroyed engines continue to smoke through the afternoon. Out over the Gulf of Carthage thunderheads are building in black anvils toward the zenith while the air grows to a perfection of stillness as if the world were an enormous room, a silent temple. The slow columns of smoke ascend through the unmoving air like prayers, while out along the black purple horizon lightning flickers.

It is almost dark before the drums are heard in the Roman camps. On the ramparts of the city they mistake it at first for the mutter of distant thunder. The rain comes on and the Carthaginian sentries stand hunched in their straw coats.

At last, out from beneath the fog of the downpour, they come, the soldiers of Rome. Along the whole dim horizon, like a slow ripple of the earth itself, the army advances: the stone carts, the slave gangs, the catapults, the engines and onagers, the auxiliaries and the heavy infantry, the mules. The columns emerge inexorably out of the obscurity, an army of the night. For the watchers on the walls there is a strange relief in this terrible vision, an unlooked for lightening of the burden of foreboding. It is the final onset. No one is deceived. There is no longer any weight of choice. There are no decisions left to be made.

44

Hanno wakes at dawn from black exhausted sleep. In the gathering day the city that emerges is the same as the city he remembers, and not the same, as if the voyagers have returned to it in a dream. The *Osiris* is the only vessel moored in that wide harbour save for a solitary barge suspended half submerged from her moorings. Mirrored rubbish hangs in the motionless water. In the city of memory the harbours were solid day and night with the world's shipping. Beyond the distant city wall three columns of smoke rise from the burnt out siege towers, vertically, like incense in a temple.

Aris the Berber has gone. He leaves in the darkness, soon after the ship is made fast to the harbour wall, taking only a length of rope and a little food. He shakes hands with Hanno and the mate.

They do not ask what his plans are. Aris is a private man, not given to unnecessary talk.

When the light of morning has grown a little, Mattho the mate leaves the ship, making his way down the abandoned dock and through the streets to find his own house in this betrayed memory of a city. On his journey through shadowed tenement canyons he passes a dead cart standing in its fuming halo of lime dust. Figures move in and out of the houses, faces masked against the stench, bringing out the dead. Ghosts watch from the darkness of doorways. Mattho is in Tartarus, a place he does not know.

He finds himself standing before the door of his own house, before the alien simulacrum of his memory, obliterated, drowned in this undergoing. The familiar details of the doorway, the worn steps, the ancient paintwork, hover behind some mystery of broken panes. As in a dream the door opens into darkness and she stands before him, eyes shining in their sockets, the ghost of herself, with a little wizened monkey at her breast, a little skeleton. She looks at him and smiles her death's head smile and turns, shuffling, and the great sobbing man stumbles after her into the darkness.

Hasdrubal's booted thugs have pushed their way through the knots of sightseers who have gathered along the dockside, and boarded the *Osiris*. They have broken open the hatches and discovered the few dozen barley sacks and the amphorae of oil in the hold, which Hanno had thought to have stowed in the ship before they departed Lilybaeum. He remonstrates reasonably and they ignore him. He does not insist. A gang of prisoners is brought up to unload the grain and the oil and Hasdrubal's men wait around bored until the work is done. Hanno broaches the topic of payment and is ignored. He does not insist.

Later that day, as he passes along the top of the sea wall with water for the sentries, Spendios sees the *Osiris* below him. It is three years since he saw the ship. He does not recognize it. If asked he would say he had never seen it before. Hanno is sitting on the deck opening nuts with a marlinspike and eating the pulverized kernels. The skeletal militiaman descends the stone steps one by one to the quay. He stands watching the tattooed face of the wild and wind-burned man as he eats. In Carthage faces are grey. Hunger has turned them grey. The barbarian looks up and beckons him aboard.

'Nut?'

Hanno passes him a handful of shelled pistachios.

'You speak like a Carthaginian.'

'There's a good reason for that.'

Spendios squats on his hams to eat the nuts. It is late afternoon. The sky over the city is grape purple. The first heavy drops make dark marks on the decking and then the rain comes on. The fogged water of the harbour hisses in the downpour. Hanno pulls across a canvas hatch-cover and they sit side by side holding it over their heads as they eat. The rain is noisy on the canvas and for a while they do not hear the drums and the trumpets. Hanno cocks his head and listens.

'What's that?'

'It is the Romans. I believe they are coming to destroy the city. I must say, you have chosen a very poor time to return to Carthage.'

Hanno gives him another handful of nuts. They eat in silence. The rain eases a little. After a time Spendios gets to his feet and dusts from his threadbare tunic the small debris of the nuts.

'That was most kind. Excellent nuts, excellent. But now I must go, I think. I must rejoin my unit. I am in the militia, you know. We have seen quite a lot of fighting recently.'

The frail, balding militiaman makes his way up the gangplank. He stands on the quay in the rain and says,

'I used to work in a library. It seems a very long time ago. Goodbye.'

Hanno watches him climb the stone steps to the wall top and make his slow way along the battlements toward the sound of the drums and the trumpets.

45

In Rome the flowers in the window boxes of the tenements are coming into bloom. The weather is warm, the air soft.

Above the cypresses that border the cemetery, white mares' tails are arabesques against the blue. Clodia looks down over her great belly into the darkness of her grandmother's grave. The old woman has ended her long conversation with the past. When she was done with her task she took to her bed. Clodia thinks how small her body seems in its linen shroud down there in the earth, no more than a glimmer in the depths of the dug grave.

It is a quiet affair, the funeral. She was a woman after all and pomp would have been unseemly, and besides she had grown to be very old. She outlived her contemporaries, her husband, even two of her own sons. Clodia is the eldest of the grandchildren. Her younger cousins are standing across from her, eyes downcast, overawed. Behind them stretches a jumbled vista of marble headstones and vaults and beyond again, between the cypresses, like a frieze, the jumbled rooftops of the Suburra rise above the old city wall. A house no bigger than a toy is on fire and she can see tiny yellow flames. A pall of smoke hangs in the distant afternoon.

Clodia sits by Cornelia's bed through the last hours, through the long sleep that ebbs by little and little to death. She listens to the ragged breathing while in her own womb the baby moves. From time to time, through the thin stuff of her shift, she catches the shape of a little heel or an elbow pushing the taut flesh of her belly. She thinks of the two souls, one waiting to leave and the other waiting to enter. She sits through the night in a chair by her grandmother and wakes suddenly to a patch of sunlight on the wall above the bed. A slave is moving about in the room putting out the lamps. About the middle of the morning the breathing stops and then starts again. She strokes the ancient, many ringed hand as it lies on the counterpane. At noon her grandmother's breathing stops and does not start again. The throat swallows and an expression of pain crosses the sleeping face.

161

Clodia sobs once, a short tearing sound like a cough almost, that she cannot contain.

Here, looking down into this black slot in the earth, Clodia is not inclined to weep. The thought of her grandmother inclines her to smile rather. She smiles for the young woman who lived on in the ancient body and for the life that she lived which was her own and which she kept as a private thing. To the world she was a Roman matron, a mother of sons, and that was her mask, the veil behind which she lived. Clodia does not think of the corpse, of the marble flesh, nor of the new life of secret rot in the crushing night black earth.

Quintus Fulvius Nobilior stands solemn and self satisfied at his young wife's side. Her condition bespeaks the fact that he has done his patriotic duty and he is pleased with the palpable evidence. They make a very republican tableau, he thinks, though in his heart of hearts he wishes his wife were taller. Her head barely reaches his shoulder. A trifle too boyish, even with her great belly. It will be a son, naturally, the child, a soldier, a Roman.

Nobilior is a fool. He is not the father of the child in her womb. Clodia has learned much from her grandmother. She has learned to live another life behind the mask. Tutilina the whore has been her teacher, her guide to the secret life. She knows the turnkeys at the prisons and gladiator schools. Clodia is fucked by criminals and prizefighters. It is her pleasure. She will not have Romans, only foreigners, Carthaginians. She has given her husband a Carthaginian baby. It is her pleasure.

Nobilior's head is bowed at the angle appropriate for the funeral of a woman, but his gaze shifts discreetly. Cornelia was old money, well-connected. The family came over with the Trojans, as the saying goes. He is wondering if there are any useful contacts to be made among the scatter of ageing patricians at the graveside.

The sexton takes up his spade. The first shovel of yellow earth makes a particular sound as it strikes the linen shroud. Clodia throws her posy of flowers into the darkness and the younger grandchildren follow her example, but she herself is suddenly lost to the moment. Beneath her dress, between her legs, she feels the hot gush of her waters breaking.

46

Torchlit barges are moved in from the sea to bridge the final stretch of water between the end of the unfinished stone causeway and the wall defending the choma. These vessels are rowed by twenty oarsmen apiece, volunteers. They creep down the coast in slow procession through the rain-black night. On the starboard side of the last of these crank barges the playwright pulls on his oar with the simple economy of his trade. It never occurred to him not to volunteer. He is a servant of the time, a witness.

Beacon fires are burning at the end of the stone spit. The flames plunge and the smoke creeps down the stones and away across the rain-pitted swell. The first pontoon is made fast to upright timbers which have been set into the end of the embankment. Each succeeding pontoon is secured to the preceding one. In the darkness the barges are jostled into line and lashed side by side. It is tricky work in the uncertain torchlight and the noise of shouting and cursing and the grinding of timbers comes out of the darkness. Archers advance from deck to deck as the undulating bridge extends closer and closer to the wall. Flights of arrows pass overhead through the falling rain. The last barge grumbles into the final space. The playwright ships his oar. He looks down through his vacant oar port into the slimy black gulf between the ship's timbers and the city wall. The gap is maybe a couple of yards wide and unseen water slaps in the depths. It is the Styx.

Even as the oarsmen hurry to make the vessel fast, the mules are struggling over the slippery rain-wet decks under the weight of the ladders, with the centurions driving them on like dogs. The first ladder goes up, swaying high over the moving void. It falls clattering across the gap to the wall. The top of the ladder scrapes about noisily on the parapet above with the movements of the barge. Infantrymen waiting on the deck are undone by the imminent prospect of what they must do.

The oarsmen hang on to the lower rungs as the fearful mules begin to climb. Stones begin to fall from the wall top. The first man on the playwright's ladder is hit and he topples like a sack into the black gulf. It is desperate work. More ladders are going up, twenty or thirty of them, and the mules begin to climb. Figures fall away, struck down by stones, but the stolid files of mechanicals do not falter. An incendiary arcs overhead and the multitudes on the ladders are thrown into livid relief. The playwright feels the deck beneath his feet listing under the weight of men and his bowels flutter. Bodies are falling. As he clings to the ladder, drowning wretches cry out from the black water below his feet.

On the top rungs the foremost mules are hacking and scrabbling blindly, locked in the simple moment. It is a place without fear, a place where everything is absent but necessity. The starved defenders, skeletons, death's men, fling themselves upon the heavily armoured mules like dervishes. It is the dance of death.

Back along the causeway, waiting under their packs, the reserve infantry columns listen with failing nerves to the cauldron roar of the fighting. The tide of noise rises and falls formlessly. The waiting troops are silent, craving some resolution, some end to insupportable listening.

Something, some descant on the roar: some new note sounds above the din, some note of exultation. There are mules on the wall top. The Carthaginians are falling back from the battlement. They are borne away, borne down, driven off; too insubstantial, too wraithlike and starved to withstand the blind, hacking onslaught. Even as he scrambles spent and panic-stricken from the wall Spendios is amazed at the *weight* of these Romans, at the terrible density of bone and muscle and iron bearing down upon them. They are driven from the wall, the skeletons. Survivors flee across the choma and through the posterns in the inner wall.

The quadrilateral is suddenly empty of defenders and the mules move out uncertainly through the silent moonlit debris. This is the foothold, this silvered expanse of ruin. Out on the mole the reserve columns are moving up. By daybreak there are four thousand Romans on the wide quadrilateral. Behind the battlements of the inner wall, the wall which guards the harbours and the citadel, wild-eyed skeletons await the renewal of the onslaught.

164

In the morning the rain stops and a blue breeze blows off the sea. Engineers are supervising the destruction of that section of the wall which gives onto the boat bridge and the causeway. Reinforcements march in through the breach and last night's assault troops are moved back to their camps to rest. They march away down the causeway past moving lines of engines, onagers, belly shooters, stone throwers, and assault towers. Through the day these engines are manoeuvred through the demolished outer defences to within a few yards of the inner wall. Behind the battlements the Carthaginians do nothing, having only stones to throw. They wait.

At daybreak of the third day the barrage begins. Within minutes the defenders are driven from the wall under the storm of steel and stone and fire, but the roaring hail does not falter. From his place by the breach in the outer wall the playwright watches dense flights of incendiaries passing over into the city and sees the strange furrowed canopy of sulphurous fog which their passing leaves. The yellow smoke leaves a taste on the tongue. Behind the wall warehouses begin to burn. Black smoke fulminates, building like a thundercloud, dimming the daylight.

About mid-morning the barrage falls suddenly silent and the assault towers move forward, crashing one after another against the wall. The infantry climb the fixed banks of ladders in columns of four, an image from a military manual, and pour unstoppably, like cockroaches, along the wall top. The defenders fall back again helplessly. They flee, comical in their feebleness, along the smoke-dark quays. The insect army of Rome pours into the city. Madness grins. The mules are everywhere, bringing fire, death and mutilation. The NCOs, the sergeants and centurions, are losing their grip. Who can resist the time? The whole quarter is burning. The empty harbours mirror the conflagration.

Hanno the sailor has remained on his ship for no better reason than that he has nowhere else to go, and there is still a little food. He shouts from his ship to the scarecrows who pass along the wharf but can get no sense. He does not know if the Romans are in the city or not. And now flaming meteors are falling out of the sky into the water and Carthaginians are flying like hail down the quay not five yards from where he stands on the deck of the *Osiris*. At the far end of the dock, warehouses are burning. Glowing fragments fall from the air like snow. He catches the distant glint of iron helmets along the wall that divides the harbours from the sea.

This is the time, these the binary and determining instants. He runs up the gangplank and casts off the mooring ropes from their iron rings. Skeletons flee helter-skelter past his elbow. Standing on the deck he poles his ship away from the quayside with all his strength. She begins to move. He runs with his pole from stem to stern, pushing her out into the fiery mirror of the harbour. Ironshirts are coming down the quay in ragged columns. Hanno hears the sound of a horn. It is the hunt and the quarry is the city. The *Osiris* glides into the still centre of the burning mirror and Hanno stands on the deck like a mariner among icebergs. Fifty yards away across the crimson lake steel helmets pass in packed, inclined ranks along the quay, leaning into the city's downfall, travellers in a storm. The sailor lets fall the stone anchors.

The Agora is the hub of the city of Carthage, a square public space flanked by temples and public altars. It lies a few streets away from the harbour district. It is the very image of opulent, far-famed Carthage. In the old days, before the war, strangers came to the Agora, travellers, foreign sailors, tourists. They stood about agog, taking in the monumental façades, the vast flags floating over gilt and vermilion altars. The tourists used to buy little bags of corn from hawkers to feed to the crowds of pigeons. They used to say that if you stand in the Agora of Carthage, the world will come to you.

It was a crowded, animated place, before the war. Files of priests passed across the paved space in an aura of tinkling bells and at certain times of the day knots of men waited for the temple whores to dance. For the men of Carthage, the native citizens, it was the place to hear the gossip and the place to be seen. Business deals were struck here, plots hatched.

Above the Agora rises the hill of the Byrsa. On hot summer days it levitates, a bleached and trembling mirage of golden rooftops.

Steep shadowed streets of tall tenements climb away from the square toward the citadel at the summit. The tourists used to wend their way up these stepped and richly odoriferous streets past souks and market stalls toward the gates of the citadel. The three streets that climb to the summit have names: Bit Kaphtor, Bit Udm, Ugar. Spendios the scribe lives with his mother on Bit Kaphtor.

Spendios used to pass through the Agora on his way to work at the city library. He used to buy bagels from a bakery just behind the temple of Melquart. In the evening on his way home he would sometimes loiter among the stalls of the second-hand book dealers in the street of the scissors grinders which runs down from the square to the old sea gate.

And now he crouches in the moon shadow among rubble where the street of the scissors grinders emerges between two temples and watches the first Roman troops as they appear with their torches at the far side of the square. They wander out into the empty space like tourists, looking about and pointing. Other gangs appear, emerging at a run from the streets that lead from the harbours. Their steps falter and they come to a halt. The lambent façades of the temples are a vision, the city of god. The mules stand on the silvered paving stones like guests. For a moment they seem no more than diminutive figures painted in as an afterthought upon the great image of the temples in the moonlight, motifs flicked in to point up the scale and majesty of the place.

The moment is short. Dacian infantry appear noisily from between the columns of the temple of Tanit. They stand swaying at the top of the temple steps, drunk. Behind them there is noise and the sound of screaming. Some of their fellows are dragging the temple whores out into the moonlight. Others stagger out from the shadows carrying gold and silver candelabras with the big altar candles still burning. A joker appears between them draped in a jewelled altar cloth, like some emperor of misrule. Out on the square there is whooping and laughter. Torches begin to move toward the temples.

Sometime around midnight Aemilianus arrives in the Agora with elements of his general staff and units of the guard. He sends the big, hatchet-faced guardsmen into the temples in search of looting infantrymen. Hapless individuals are dragged before the general. He has them executed on the spot. Something approaching order is restored.

Gates have been opened in the city wall by the harbours and new troops march past the still burning warehouses and up the echoing streets to the Agora. These fresh troops are posted under arms at all points around the square from which a counter attack might be made.

Through the night the rubble-strewn streets are loud with the tramp of nailed boots and by the time the light of day is beginning to gather, the square is already a vista of infantrymen.

High up, the first misty rays of the sun strike the gilded domes of the Citadel. The golden vision shimmers like a sign in the sky. The slopes of the Byrsa are still in shadow and the steep streets that lead to the summit are vertical gulfs of darkness. The tenements brood silently. There are no lights in the windows. There is no movement.

The streets leading to the summit climb parallel to one another. Aemilianus sits his horse where these narrow streets leave the Agora watching as the columns form up. He does not know if these men will encounter resistance. The signs are good. Nothing moves. There are no barricades. He thinks that maybe the Guggas are preparing a last defence of the citadel on the summit. He looks up toward the golden rooftops. This is the way, the route he must take. These streets are the shortest path to his goal. He raises his hand.

The dressed columns move off in step as if this place were a parade ground. The crash of boots echoes hugely as they pass into the shadow. Aemilianus catches the bob and glint of steel helmets as his troops go up between the sombre cliffs of stone.

When it comes, the deluge of stones from the rooftops and windows is sudden and terrible. Whole parapets and chimneystacks topple into the void. The brisk columns are obliterated. The cobbled way is instantly thick with the dead and dying. Those who are still whole crouch in doorways or press themselves against the walls. Dust from the descending rubble billows from the street end into the square and the noise of screaming rises above the thunder of the downpour. Survivors stumble out from this hell's mouth, white-eyed and moaning.

Aemilianus does not flinch. His face is set. He does not wait. He orders units of the guard into the first buildings in each of the streets to flush out the defenders. They go at a run, carrying their shields over their heads. They batter down the doors and tear away the tall shutters from the windows, pressing and scrambling through into dark interiors. They disappear inside and for the troops who are watching from the square there follow moments of imminence in which nothing seems to happen. The shutters of a first floor window burst open and a child arcs into the street below. A woman follows, and another child, fiddling the air. A cheer goes up from the spectators in the Agora. At the windows there are glimpses of movement as the struggle passes from floor to floor, but progress seems slow. What is keeping them? From a fifth floor window a guardsman falls backward into the gulf still clutching his opponent. Another wait. At last a guardsman's helmet can be seen moving about on the flat rooftop.

This is the pattern. The tenement buildings are defended, every one. Each is a fortress and every stairway and every landing and doorway is contested. The defenders have nothing. They fight with swords recovered from Roman dead, with chair legs and kitchen knives and pans of boiling water. They retreat floor by floor and when those who are left alive are finally driven to the rooftop they make rickety bridges of planks and ceiling joists over the alleyways and cross to the next fortress. In the streets below, the mules look up at the skeletons creeping over the void.

It is slow work and as darkness falls, only six or seven of the buildings at the bottom ends of the three streets have been occupied. Losses have been heavy in the stinking stairwells. The narrow, stepped thoroughfares climb interminably toward the distant summit. The task will take weeks.

Aemilianus will brook no delay. The army is the hammer with which he means to forge his victory, his fame. He has the patrician's necessary gift of oblivion to the sufferings of lesser men. He orders the exhausted troops out and fresh troops are sent back in immediately. Rotas are organized: troops will be deployed in shifts.

The fighting goes on through the night. Torches move in the black defiles. There is shouting and screaming in the darkness. The mules come to hate this night fighting, when the corkscrew stairwells are black dark, and mad eyed scarecrows creep unseen. They learn to stay together in the torchlight. Empty rooms are full of horror. Whole squads perish on rooftops, burned to death in fires that have been purposely lit on floors below.

On the second morning of the assault, Aemilianus orders up teams of sappers with pickaxes and crowbars. They begin demolishing the cleared houses. As the first tall curtain of masonry falls away, the debris is full of floor timbers and furniture and household goods. It also contains the living, those who have been hiding in cupboards and sealed rooms. They move feebly in the smoking fans of fallen wreckage.

Sappers are ordered forward to buildings which are still occupied, but this is desperate work and the defenders attack them with stones from upper windows. Archers are brought up to cover the windows. Auxiliaries are set to work clearing the debris from the cobbled thoroughfares so that troops can pass and the wounded and the dead can be brought out. The mules are brought up in shifts, twelve hours on, twelve hours off. When their time is over they trudge out of the burning maw, dust-grey, exhausted. They pass by the incoming troops without speaking.

Stories circulate among the troops, of tripwires and sections of upper stairways rigged to collapse, of fools lured into empty rooms by a glimpse of naked flesh and garrotted behind the door, of madmen setting themselves on fire and hurling themselves down upon their enemies, of feral infants in abandoned rooms gnawing the bones of the dead. They will dream of this place until they die.

At the bottoms of each of these contested streets some joker has daubed street names from Rome. Vicus Tuscus, Via Flaminia, Boararium. The Boararium is the meat market. Whores loiter on Flaminia. The joke embedded in Tuscus is obscure. It is where the rich go to do their shopping.

Spendios is craning over the parapet. Six stories down, the street is a milling mass of troops though he cannot see clearly for the drifting smoke. The building across the way is on fire and figures on the flat rooftop move about in a mirage of rising heat. Through the wavering air he can see Qart standing on the parapet, a thin man with pale hair, calm, untouched. He is helping fellow fugitives onto the bridge of boards that hangs over the alley. Spendios had thought him dead, like so many of the others. He cannot remember how many.

He looks down into the smoking chasm which used to be the street where he lived for so many years, the place he returned to each day, Bit Kaphtor. It is another country.

The bottom half of the street has gone. It is a desolation of mounds where fires burn. They are pulling the tenements down as they advance. He can see files of helmets moving up, threading their way between the rubble hills. Out over the city there are fires burning as far as he can see. The warehouses down by the harbours have been burning for days. The solitary ship floats at anchor in the harbour, a magic toy. For a second he sees the face of the tattooed man.

Spendios is blank, exhausted, dying. If they do not kill him, he says, he will die anyway. His body is bones. In the lulls between onslaughts, he sleeps, anywhere, on a stair, in the corner of an empty room, going down like a stone through dark waters, and when he is shaken awake he is numb and stupid. He has no memory of another time.

Next to Spendios the widow Mara is shouting and pointing down to the foot of the building where they stand. Spendios is looking about at the paved rooftop, and it comes to him in an odd epiphany that this is where he lives, this building.

He looks about in a kind of amazement at the litter of broken urns where once he grew flowers. He used to hang his washing up here on this roof.

And now he is here, at last. He has come home, fleeing across the rooftops. In a shuttered room of the floor below, his mother is sitting in her chair, waiting. She cannot move from her chair, being too weak, but sits by the closed shutters with the slatted light falling across her face.

He has tried to get back each day, to lift her from the chair to the pot, to make sure she has water in her cup to drink. He smoothes the blanket over her knees and kisses her. He cannot remember when he last saw her. Was it this morning? Yesterday? He has lost track. He must go now.

'See! See! There by the corner.'

Mara is shaking his arm. Through the flying smoke he glimpses a huddle of sappers on the cobbles below as they lever away a stone doorframe from the wall. A little avalanche of masonry spills into the road as the stone column falls. On the roof, they feel the tremor. Roman infantrymen are tumbling out of the building.

'I told you! It's about to go! They're clearing the building. Come, now.'

Mara is pushing Spendios toward the bridge over the alley. The stone slabs under their feet blur as the tenement moves and they fall down together among broken flowerpots, and then she is on her knees dragging him toward the bridge.

'Come! Come! We can live!'

Tears are running down his face. He helps her over the low wall. She is standing on the plank bridge, still holding his hand. Below her feet is the smoking void. Spendios is still on the other side of the low parapet.

'Come.'

She is looking at him, on the edge of panic.

'Come. What? What's the matter?'

He makes a small movement with his head and closes his eyes for long moment. Tears run out beneath his eyelids.

'This is my house, you see. I am standing on the roof of my own house. This is where we live, mother and I. She is downstairs. She may need a drink. She may need to use the toilet.'

The building jolts and Mara grips his hand to prevent herself falling. She is looking into his face and he is nodding at her foolishly and smiling.

'I have to lift her, you understand.'

He nods and smiles, urging her to go with his bright tearful smile. She glances to the rooftop across the alley. The building lurches and dust pulses out between the stone slabs of the terrace. She clutches his hand and arm. She sees that he will not come over the parapet. She turns away. He watches her go, arms out from her body for balance, teetering out over the chasm. She stumbles forward against the low wall at the far side and scrambles over.

Across the twilit room his mother is sitting in her chair with the bars of light falling across her face. Her voice is a memory of itself, a slight papery sound.

'You're late.'

'We have to go, mother.'

'Go? Where will we go?'

He puts his arms beneath her and lifts her from the chair as if she were a bundle of rags. She has wet herself.

'We shall go away, mother, away from here.'

The room falters and he staggers, holding her in his arms. Plaster falls as a sudden zig zag of daylight splits the wall. He takes a step toward the door and the room moves again. In front of him the floor opens up so that he can see into the burning room below. Great spears of daylight slice through the walls as they split apart. The whole corner of the room begins to arc slowly out over the void. As it goes down into the pit, Spendios the scribe is still standing with his mother in his arms.

47

Clinging in the darkness to the cross tree of the *Osiris*, Hanno can see out over the burning city. To the North, the whole slope of the new town is ablaze. The crowded monuments of the cemeteries stand in black relief against the glare. The streets that run up to the Byrsa are corridors of fire and the gilded domes of the citadel flicker redly behind the rising smokes. He cannot tell if the citadel has fallen. He wonders what has become of the man who came and ate his pistachio nuts.

Hanno climbs the mast of the ship every few hours to watch the destruction of Carthage. He is in a sort of limbo, anchored in the middle of the harbour. It is as if he were invisible. He makes no attempt to hide himself from the Roman troops who pass continuously in both directions along the quay. Yesterday the first columns of prisoners began passing out of the city to the slave ships. Starving, no more than living skeletons, they will fetch nothing at the auctions of Delos. And today, from the masthead he could just make out columns of carts moving out through the Taenia Gate, the first of the loot from temple treasuries he guesses.

He exists in his limbo, on the deck of his landlocked ship, a becalmed mariner. He has no feelings, being only a mirror to the time, except fear, and hunger. What little food Hasdrubal's men did not take has gone and the water in the cask is brackish, hardly drinkable and leaves him thirstier than if he had not drunk at all.

Hanno has a plan, a sort of a plan. Tomorrow, because he cannot swim, he will cut the anchor cable and work the ship with the steering oar across to the quay on the west side of the harbour. If he can see from the mast top more carts passing out through the gate, he will slip over the dock wall, through the Tophet precinct and join the procession of vehicles. That is as far as his plan goes. He has half persuaded himself that the carters will be civilians. He is very frightened. Tomorrow he may be dead or on his way into slavery.

It works better than he could have hoped. He watches the passing column of carts from the shadow of an alley. He falls in behind an overloaded ox cart and begins walking out of his native city, uneasily aware of the driver of the cart behind him. The streets are strewn with every kind of rubbish. The besieged city was given over long ago to dereliction and decay. At an intersection a boarded up shop is burning but otherwise there is no sign of life. Whoever lived in these streets has fled.

At the gate a company of Dacians are posted. They stand about, bored and sullen. There are civilian administrators sitting at trestle tables arguing with shippers and contractors. The business of emptying the dying city of its portable wealth has already begun.

As Hanno is passing under the gate there is some kind of commotion and the cart in front of him comes to a halt. He stops, uncertain what he should do, tense with anxiety, breathing shallowly in and out, willing the cart to move again. He glances back to the driver of the cart behind, who is rummaging under his seat. A clerk pushes past him waving a list and shouting at someone he cannot see.

What Hanno does not know is that it occurs to no one that he is a Carthaginian. News of the imminent fall of the city has brought shippers, carpetbaggers and opportunists of every stripe to the

Roman camps. This one is obviously a foreigner, with his tattooed face. He looks too well fed, in any case, for a Gugga.

The cart in front of him creaks into motion and he walks on again in its shadow, out of his native city. He looks back across the sand for a moment to the city wall. The long procession of vehicles is bumping along the cobbled way which the Romans have built along the sandy coast. Ahead the beach is a vista of activity. Here and there carts are leaving the column and turning down toward the water. In the offing, an assortment of transports and merchant ships ride at anchor, Sicilian hippoi, much like the *Osiris*, Italian galleys, Delian slavers, and military transports. Smaller craft move out and back ferrying material from the shore.

In the shallows, some kind of statue wrapped in sacking is being manhandled by half a dozen sailors onto a makeshift raft. There is a commotion as the raft tilts and the statue slides beneath the water. Crates are stacked here and there near the sea's edge and people are moving about, shippers, sailors, and tallymen. Hanno's anxiety lifts a little. This is a form of life he recognises. There are chances here, possibilities. He leaves the column of carts and walks down to the water.

A ship's boat is approaching the shore. Sailors leap into the shallows, dragging her up the shingle. The merchant who has been sitting in the stern stands up unsteadily. He stands there in his embroidered burnous and his overstated gold jewellery, waiting to be carried to the sand. He is a big man and the sailor who wades over to him staggers as the merchant climbs onto his back. The wretch takes a step, stumbles, and both men go down into the water. The doused merchant splashes out of the water spluttering with parodic rage. He is wringing water from the hems of his sopping robe.

'Stupid, stupid sod! Do you know how much this cost? Have you any idea, you, you arse?'

He has a gold earring in the shape of a snake and an eye patch. He is fatter than Hanno remembers him. It is Yassib, the shipper of lions.

48

Yassib waves his hand at the houseboy and drinks appear on a silver tray: a silver decanter and long stemmed glasses. The years have been good to him. The view from the window of his Sicilian villa takes in the sunset over the sea. Hanno sits in a clean, borrowed tunic, bathed, fed, released. He looks out across the darkening sea. Over the empty horizon Carthage is in its death throes. He sits in a kind of amazement that this can be so. Over the horizon tens of thousands are going into the pit. There is a world on fire, a world of horror and madness just out of sight over the horizon, while he sits, sipping expensive wine on an overstuffed couch. Chance broods at his elbow. A profound bewilderment that is close to despair darkens his vision. Yassib's voice seems to come from far away.

'Where was I? The books, that's right. It was a funny contract, money for old rope in the end. He was an Egyptian, oldish bloke, some bigwig from the library in Alexandria. Books, books out of Carthage, whatever I could get, as many as I could get. That was it. Well, I looked at him old fashioned and he said that he thought the Romans were going to destroy the city totally, that they would erase all memory of its existence. He said that they would burn all of the libraries and that as a librarian he felt a duty to do what he could. His superiors had voted him the means. That's what he said, that they had voted him the means. Those were his exact words. He meant the money, and he had a lot of money, I can tell you. We did a deal, so much per volume, whatever we could get. Well, I got connections, obviously, and I sent a message to a certain party on the general staff at Carthage offering certain financial inducements and he sent a written order to one of his field officers who was in charge of one of the demolition parties, and out they came, thousands of them, cartloads. I've never seen so many books, and every one of them worth ready money. We was just loading the last of the crates when you walked down that beach like a painted heathen. I kept a few. I don't know why. I don't even know what they're about.'

Yassib reaches under the low table and fishes out a book. He reads the title page.

'Look at this. *A Compendium of Horticulture. Volume Nine.*'

He opens it at random and reads. A few grains of millet fall from between the pages.

'Chapter twelve. On the cultivation of figs.'

He drops the book to the floor and pours himself another drink.

'I moved out of the wild animal trade before the war. Well, I moved out of Carthage, didn't I. I've got this place now, and I've got a place in Spain, a farm, olive groves. I hardly get there.

You could see it coming. You could see it a mile off, and me being in the wild animal business I spent a lot of time in Rome, a lot, in those days, before the war. You get the feel of things, and it felt bad, I can tell you. Everybody knew.

They're unstoppable. Who's going to stop them? What they did in Greece, some of it was horrible.

Carthage was different. I've got a theory. Think of all those senators in Rome, all those politicians that pull the strings, well they're old see, sixty, seventy, eighty some of them. That old bugger that died just before the war, Cato, he was eighty odd. The whole city turned out for his funeral, even though they all hated the old bastard.

Anyway, think about it. They must have been kids, those senators, little boys, when Hannibal was in Italy all those years ago. He was in Italy for years, what was it, twelve years, more maybe, and he frightened the shit out of the Romans. He fucked them over time after time, the Ticino, the Trebbia, Trasimene, Cannae. They thought they'd had it. Every family had somebody killed. Imagine it, all those mothers and grandmothers and nurses, frightened witless and clinging on to the little ones. Imagine all those little boys wetting their beds and crying in the night because they think one-eyed Hannibal is coming to get them. And it went on for years, you know, the fear. I bet some of them still wet the bed.

And then, fifty years on, all those little boys are running the world. The legions can't be stopped. They're everywhere, Greece, Macedon, Spain, Sicily. They're not frightened of one-eyed Hannibal now. This time they're not just going to beat Carthage, they're going to obliterate it, smear it from the face of the earth.

They're going to show them. They're going to show everybody. Delenda est Carthago. Carthage has gone. It doesn't exist.'

Hanno is crying. Great tears are flowing down his face. He has gone out into the tragedy of the destruction of the city. The burden of survival has descended upon him.

49

It is said that in the days of its prosperity a million people lived in the city of Carthage, within the twenty-mile circuit of its outer wall. With the first falling of the shadow of Rome upon the place and even before, maybe two or three years or even longer than that before the purposes of the Roman Senate became clear, there were those who knew. Spendios the scribe knew. Some, unlike the scribe, trusted their intuitions and left. Merchants with agents in every port of the inland sea, closed up their Carthage offices. Assets were moved to Tyre, Sidon, Delos, Egypt. As the times darkened, this subtle and unremarked bleeding away became an anxious exodus, mostly of the rich. Even after the war began and the armies of Rome were camped at the gates it was still possible to get away, if you had the right connections, and the money, though there were always those who knew that it would all blow over. Arrad the moneylender knew that it would blow over. Everything blows over.

With the coming of the war many of those living outside, fled within the walls of Carthage. These were farmers, peasants, poor folk from the city's hinterland, frightened away by the brutalities of the Roman foraging parties and the terrors of the times. The wise ones left the provinces of the city altogether and moved away along the coast to Numidia or Libya. Those not so wise moved into the city. They colonized houses abandoned by the wealthy and built their shanties in the empty gardens.

There were deserters too, Romans, Gauls, Dacians, those who had fallen foul of the iron discipline of the army of the republic. They gave themselves up at the gates and were drafted into the militia groups.

178

With the return of Hasdrubal into the city, flight from Carthage was declared treasonable, a capital offence. The exodus of the living came to a halt – though one gate from the city always stood open, a dark portal, and during the long months of want and starvation, many left through that exit. No one knows how many died in the fighting on the walls, or how many were executed for treasonable offences against the state. No one knows how many died from sickness and starvation. The tally of those deaths grew greater from month to month. In the final weeks there were few burials and the dead lay rotting in alleyways and in rooms noisy with flies. In the last days death was a friend.

And now the city is burning end to end and all of the defenders who remain alive are confined within the walls of the temple precinct on the summit of the Byrsa. The walls are ancient and massive. A flight of sixty steps leads up to the gate of the precinct and though many of the defenders must be close to death, it is not clear to the Romans how the place is to be taken at last. The enormous labour of bringing up a siege train is hardly to be contemplated. Aemilianus issues an amnesty. He will spare the lives of those who give themselves up and they will be sold into slavery.

In his history of the war, Appianus writes that fifty thousand people surrendered under that amnesty, one twentieth part of the city's original population. Among that number are Mattho the mate of the *Osiris*, his wife and one surviving child, and Mara the widow.

It takes a whole morning for this scarecrow multitude to pass down through the gate of the sanctuary. It is a spectacle beyond the reach of pity. The playwright stands among the silent mules, watching.

The sanctuary gate closes behind the last departing ghost and the bars can be heard dropping into place. A few hundred remain inside, diehards, patriots, idealists, the mad. Some are deserters from the army of Rome who wish to avoid the regulation punishment for their offence: crucifixion. Hasdrubal's wife and her children are among those who do not quit the place. Her husband, the commander, cannot be found.

The end, the enactment of the end, is not long delayed. There is an open square in front of the steps which ascend to the sanctuary gate, a paved space where tall palms were once grown to give pilgrims shade after the long climb from the city below. There was a drinking fountain set into a wall with brass cups on chains, but the fountain is dry, the cups gone.

A raised dais has been set up across from the gate and lines of troops in some semblance of dress uniform are drawn up behind it. Centurions take their places to either side carrying the eagles of the legions. Scarecrows begin to appear along the battlement above the gate. Smoke is rising behind them into the sky: the sanctuary is on fire.

The commander-in-chief walks across the square to the dais and sits with his Consular baton across his knee. The times have wrought their changes upon him. His youth has fled. He is no longer the darling of the army, the boy wonder. His face is fixed, hardly human, a tic flicking at the corner of his mouth. His name is terror.

He sits in silence looking out across the empty square to the gate. The dull roar of the fire inside the sanctuary can be heard and snaking flames are beginning to rise behind the battlement, throwing the scarecrows into black relief.

Aemilianus raises his hand and out from between the lines of stony faced troops a comic figure is hustled, a fat clown. Hasdrubal is pushed forward into the space. They have stripped him naked and painted his flesh white. He carries an olive branch. He turns this way and that as if unsure of his whereabouts. High above him the scarecrows are screaming and gesticulating like figures in some allegorical painting of the damned.

The tall doors of the sanctuary begin to swing inward, framing the inferno within, and out of the glare walks Hasdrubal's wife with her two children. She stands in the gateway at the top of the flight of steps, composed and still, holding the children against her body.

It is a time and a place, you would think, for speeches, for tragic rhetoric, but nothing is said. Hasdrubal becomes aware of her as he stands below her in his lonely circus ring, and then his glance flickers toward Aemilianus.

In the moment that his gaze shifts to the general's dais his wife kills the elder of their children, their son, slitting his throat with a dagger. The little girl runs away but her mother catches up with her before she reaches the edge of the steps. She falls to the ground with the child at the very brink, stabbing repeatedly. When she stands up again, it is plain to see that her body is trembling violently and she staggers as she tries to catch up the blood sodden hems of her gown. It seems for a moment that she may fall down the stone steps but she recovers herself. Her spine is straight as she walks back through the gate and into the fire. The child's body shudders a little then lies still.

50 ·

The work of destruction is going on everywhere, the burning and demolition. The mules work stripped to the waist like day labourers, their mouths covered against the pestilential stink. There is no need for armour or weapons. The streets that are still standing are deserted, uncanny places. Nothing moves, not a cat or a dog. Looted temples stand empty and silent. The superstitious mules are uneasy. The people of Carthage are dead or gone. From time to time some famished skeleton is found cowering in a cellar or a cistern. A few armed guards oversee the slave battalions who are being kept on to help in the work of destroying their own city, before being shipped off to the mines and the auctions.

Every building within the twenty mile circuit of the walls is to be pulled down, every tree felled and burned. Offices have been set up in empty buildings with street maps covering the walls. Clerks cross off the districts as they are destroyed. Thoroughness is all.

Civil engineers are brought out from Rome to supervise the demolition of the larger public buildings and a deputation of senior senators has arrived to advise Aemilianus on the administration of the peace in Africa.

The city walls themselves are gnawed away, as it might be, by termites. Even the great triple wall that stretches for three thousand yards across the isthmus, with its massive towers and cavernous barracks built within the thickness of the masonry, has been reduced to isolated promontories of stone. They stare out, these broken cliffs of masonry, over the desert that is Africa. The mules grow sullen as the weeks pass and the city districts are reduced one by one to lunar landscapes of bitter rubble, oppressed by the monstrousness of the task.

Knots of sightseers begin to appear, mostly rich people who have chartered boats from Ostia or Lilybaeum. Young staff officers conduct them around the ruins. They gather mementoes from the debris, a human jawbone with a gold tooth still in its socket, a burned book, a broken brooch. These things will be passed round the table as curiosities at dinner parties on the Palatine.

The playwright wanders the dead city each day, returning only in the darkness to the camps, and he is back in the burning streets again before it grows light. It is the wasteland, infernal, without hope. It will give him no rest and he cannot be quit of it. It draws him like a holy place.

In his wanderings through this necropolis he comes upon the corpse of Arrad the moneylender sprawled across the threshold of his house. A single coin glints between his clenched fingers. Across the street, his head lies in the gutter, his open eyes fixed on nothing. The last frenzied prayers, the loosening of his bowels, have passed and both parts of the moneylender lie quietly now. His body has entered into a new life. His body has gone out into the world, has become the world: he is the multitude. Flies' eggs lie in the ends of the severed arteries of his neck and on the filmy iris of his eye. In his putrefying body cavity new cities have been founded where teeming millions labour.

The drone of flies is everywhere, a sound transcending other sounds, like a sound in the mind.

In a moonscape of rubble hills the playwright comes across Spendios and his mother, dust grey statues, half buried in a slope of bricks. He is still holding her in his arms though she is cruelly crushed.

In blackened streets, in the ash of the firestorm, bodies lie like charred wood, remote as effigies. The playwright steps over them as he passes.

Fires are burning everywhere.

In streets and alleys where the fires have not raged, the ground underfoot is thick with drifts of trampled trash: shoes, smashed crockery, cutlery, tools, ash, broken glass, books, children's toys, flattened baskets, rags of clothing, mats made from jute and woven palm, beads, chair legs. For yards together this carpet of debris conceals the cobbled roadway beneath. It is the soil in which seeds will take root, willow herb and ox-eyed daisy. In a few weeks the first flowers will open.

He picks up a shoe that lies at his feet, half buried in the rubbish. It is a child's shoe, the sole worn to a hole, an unremarkable object, just one among a million relics of time, objects that cannot speak, cannot give voice to the torment of the time. They are like the dead, these abandoned things: their time is past. He holds the shoe against his body, rocking and bereft.

High in the sky, hardly to be seen through the drifting fogs of ruin, swallows are passing northward.

51

Clodia watches the baby suck, its navy blue eyes fixed on nothing. The pain in the sucked breast ebbs slowly away and she falls into her reverie of accomplishment. It is what she loves most, the drawing down of the milk. She is engulfed by her new condition as a person with two lives. It is a girl: Cornelia, after her grandmother.

She is sitting on the terrace of her new house on the Palatine. It is a warm spring afternoon, though she has a blanket over knees because everyone insisted, and because these are the days of her confinement and such things are customary. Dappled sunlight races about on the grass as the umbrella pines move in the breeze. Above the trees, high in the blue spring sky, swallows are passing northward.

She is a Roman matron now, with a child, a house and slaves of her own. Nobilior wants his wife to use a wet nurse but she will have none of it. Her husband is not quite happy that he has sired a daughter, and not a son. If only he knew.

Her tiny Carthaginian has stopped sucking and lies in the crook of her arm in a little trance, its eyes unblinking, until she touches its cheek with her fingertip and it begins again with a start.

A letter has arrived from Aemilianus. He writes each month and for a time she found that she looked forward to his stuffy letters from Carthage, though she is not sure why. He writes a lot about food supplies, about morale, discipline and the need for a clearly understood system of punishment in the legions. She knows from what she hears, because the war is all that Nobilior her husband talks about, the war and his patriotic duty, that it will end soon and that the Carthaginians will be beaten.

What Clodia looks for in these dutiful letters, what she likes best, is not news of the war itself, but the slips, the little leakages of the personal into what he writes. She has a sort of collection in her head of the things he has written that have made her smile, forms of words that have conjured him up as a person. I have had problems with my bowels is her favourite.

His letters seem to have grown more pompous since he went back last year as Consul, as if they were intended for his official biographer, which they probably are. Clodia has been careful to keep the letters.

She picks up the letter from the tray by her chair, slides her finger under the seal and unfolds the heavy paper. She skims the usual polite enquiries about her health and the family. She looks at the page. There is something about the writing itself, the black ranks of letters, which is new. The writing, usually so firm and legible, is hatched and hasty. Agitation comes off the page like vapour. She begins to read.

The city has fallen after three years. The fighting in the streets lasted a week and losses were heavy. I have obeyed the orders that were given to me. I have exterminated the Carthaginian people and now I have set the army to the task of destroying the material city – as I have been ordered to do. The work will take some weeks.

I am told that my career in Rome is now assured. Our successes in Africa cannot but help the fortunes of the family. Naturally I will be granted a Triumph when I return to Rome.

Yesterday I watched a Carthaginian woman kill her own children — a shocking act of blasphemy. Last night I did not sleep. Whatever may happen in the future please remember sister that I have been acting under orders throughout and that everything that has been done here has been done in the name of the Senate and the Roman people.

She folds up the letter, unable to read on. The baby stirs at her breast, writhes a little, then settles again to suck, sinking back into that primal dream of plenitude. The tiny balled fists uncurl.

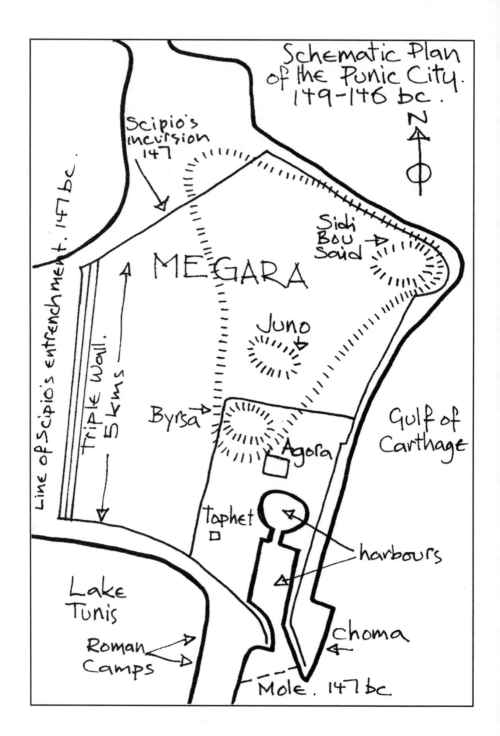

Schematic Plan of the Punic City. 149–146 bc.

N

Scipio's incursion 147

Line of Scipio's entrenchment. 147 bc.

Triple Wall. 5 kms

MEGARA

Sidi Bou Said

Juno

Byrsa

Agora

Gulf of Carthage

Tophet

harbours

Lake Tunis

Roman Camps

choma

Mole. 147 bc

Note

The Greek historian Polybius, who according to his own account, was present at the fall of Carthage, afterwards wrote a forty volume history of Rome. Of the forty volumes, the first five survive complete but none of them concern the fall of Carthage. The rest are lost, or almost. Fragments survive in epitomes and collections that were compiled about a thousand years after Polybius' death. Of these fragments only three relate to the third Punic War: maybe five or six pages in all.

The nearest thing to a source text, indeed the only extant source, apart from Polybius, relating to the third Punic War, is Appianus' Roman History which was written maybe three hundred years after the event. In that part of his history which deals with the fall of Carthage, Appianus quotes briefly from one of the lost books of Polybius. It is a matter of speculation whether other sources may have been available to Appianus. The question of how heavily he relied on the lost sections of Polybius' account remains open.

The scores of more recent histories which devote themselves wholly or in part to the third Punic War derive entirely from these two sources. Archaeological evidence exists though it is scant.

Anyone reading Appian and Polybius will see that in writing my own book there have been times when I have deliberately side-stepped the source texts and rearranged things to suit my own purposes, whatever they might be, and I have in any case ignored the greater part altogether in order to include other things.

Josephus' dubious account of the fall of Jerusalem, which he witnessed in AD 70, makes riveting reading and conjures up the vision of a city under siege. Plutarch's life of Cato was also useful.

There is nothing at all scrupulous about what I have written, but nothing unscrupulous either. It is a work of fiction.

The extant writings of Polybius which relate to the fall of Carthage exist in translation in the Loeb Classical Library (*Polybius' Histories. Vol. 6*) as does Appianus' account. (*Appian's Roman History. Vol. 1*). Serge Lancel's history of Carthage (*Carthage: A History*. Trans.

Antonia Nevill. Blackwell.) is the best and most complete history of the city I have come across and includes much recent archaeological data.

I include the following details for anyone with a taste for such esoterica: For the five extant books of Polybius' histories the definitive surviving manuscript is *A, Codex Vaticanus 124,* an eleventh century text. Fragments of the lost volumes are to be found in *F, Codex Urbinas 102* in the *Constantine Exerpts* and in *M, Codex Vaticanus 73,* a palimpsest of the tenth century.

A possible Chronology

264-241   First Punic War.

218-201   Second Punic War.

152   Cato's embassy to Africa.
             Carthage makes the last of 50 annual war
             reparations payments to Rome. Carthage attacks
             Numidia. Hasdrubal the general in command of this
             expedition is sentenced to death on his return to
             Carthage. He flees. Utica defects to Rome.
             Roman forces under consuls Censorinus and
             Manilius assemble in Sicily. Punic embassy to
             Rome. 300 hostages are handed over.

149   Spring. Roman army disembarks in Utica.
             Carthage hands over its armaments to Rome.
             Announcement to 30 Cathaginian elders that the
             city is to be destroyed. Elders are killed on their
             return to the city. Attacks on resident Italians.
             Slaves freed. Hasdrubal pardoned.

             Summer. Manilius launches attacks on the triple
             wall. Censorinus attacks the wall to the South.
             Carthage abandoned by Hadrumentum, Lepsis,
             Acholla. Operations outside the city against
             Hasdrubal.

148   Scipio settles Masinissa's Numidian succession and
             returns to Carthage with Numidian army under
             Gulussa. Phameas, Hasdrubal's lieutenant defects
             to Rome with 2,000 cavalry. New consuls elected:
             L. Calpurnius Piso, L. Hostilius Mancinus.
             Attacks on Cap Bon. Neapolis sacked.

147	Spring. Mancinus' abortive incursion over the city wall to the North is relieved by Scipio Aemilianus, recently returned as Commander-in-Chief. Incursion into the suburb of Megara. Hasdrubal comes within the walls, improves the city's defences. Scipio builds trenched camp across isthmus. Construction of mole to close off the harbours begins. Carthage opens entrance in sea wall allowing ships to emerge. An inconclusive sea battle ensues. Night attack against the engines on the mole. Autumn. 4,000 men on quadrilateral. Nepheris sacked.
146	Spring. Carthage taken by storm.

For a full list of our publications please write to

Dewi Lewis Publishing
8 Broomfield Road
Heaton Moor
Stockport SK4 4ND

You can also visit our web site at

www.dewilewispublishing.com